GINGERSNAP

ODIN'S FURY MOTORCYCLE CLUB
BOOK FOUR

VICTORIA JAYNE

LIMITLESS
PUBLISHING

GINGERSNAP

Limitless Publishing, LLC
Kailua, HI 96734
www.limitlesspublishing.com

Formatting: Limitless Publishing

ISBN-13: 978-1-64034-630-7

DEDICATION

For my amazing husband. Thank you for always being in my corner, reminding me never to forget my wins, and to stop focusing on my losses. Ghost and Shy, words cannot express how grateful I am to have you in my life. Lastly, Booktok After Dark, thank you for all your love and support.

CHAPTER 1

Dash

*P*arties at the clubhouse had the potential to get wild. They were often rowdy. With Aerosmith's *Toys in the Attic* album playing on the speaker, Dash's brothers drank to the memory of their president. The only drinks served that night were Bowie's favorites: Wild Turkey bourbon and Miller Lite. While these were not Dash's favorite drinks, he would enjoy them and the time with his brothers.

For now, it was just members of the club, no hang arounds, no club whores, no Ol' Ladies. Just men with a rocker. Prospects took up their posts at the door and behind the bar. Drinks were flowing as easily and swiftly as the memories of Bowie.

As the afternoon turned into evening and the men got drunker, their need for entertainment kicked in. The club sluts trickled through the door, welcomed by both in-state and out-of-state brothers. The tone of the evening shifted away from mourning and more toward the celebration of Bowie's life and memory.

A few of the Ol' Ladies made their way to the clubhouse and Dash watched as Sparrow sought out Romeo. His young club brother, since hooking up with her, never indulged in the free pussy thrown at him. As a legacy patch, with much higher ranks in his future, Romeo was targeted by many a thirsty bitch who wanted that ride.

Loyalty was a code his brothers lived by. Now, that didn't necessarily mean that loyalty extended to the women. Even when a guy claimed one as his Ol' Lady, he may still dick around with club ass. Loyalty was expected to be to the club and to his brothers, anything else was inconsequential. Not Romeo, though. He was only interested in his wild-haired lollipop-loving girl.

As he switched his focus, he noted a few other men greeting their women. Each woman wore her property vest proclaiming to whom they belonged. Each also had a nickname stitched on it, their equivalent to the road names of the men. Dash, Romeo, Clark, Monty—none of those were their given, legal names. His lip pulled up slightly and he shook his head. Dash couldn't remember the last time someone called him by his given name.

That realization made him think of Gingersnap, and her proper name. Sipping his bourbon, he stared off, watching Blue, topless, straddling Mooky as he licked a shot off her tits. He didn't know Blue's actual name, nor did he care to. Gingersnap—he wanted to know her name. He wanted to know more about her, all about her.

Maybe it was the bourbon, maybe it was his survivor's guilt again, but Dash slid off his barstool, slapped Cajun on the back, and headed toward the back door. Pulling both his phone and his cigarettes from his pocket, he decided it was time to know more about Gingersnap, but he wanted to focus. Sitting in a bustling clubhouse with tits and ass a plenty, plus so many people talking, there'd be no way he could concentrate.

With a cigarette hanging from his lip, he exited the party. Cool air slapped him in the face as he stepped outside. The door closed behind him, muffling *Cherry Pie* by Warrant as he dropped his bulky frame onto one of the patio chairs.

PRK

Lotion?

He sparked his lighter, puffing his cigarette to life. Tilting his head upward, he looked up at the passing clouds as he exhaled a long stream of smoke.

GINGERSNAP

Done already. How are you doing?

Of course she did it already. She was smart and obedient. The lotion wasn't just an assignment. It would help her skin heal and decrease any risks of scarring.

PRK

I'm all right. How are you?

Shaking his head, he pulled his cigarette from his lips and mentally kicked himself. He wanted to be in contact with her but had nothing to say. Considering he never engaged in idle chit chat with his play partners, this felt awkward for him. He never concerned himself talking to the previous women when they weren't playing because he never wanted any sort of connection with them. Resting his phone on his knee, he pinched at the bridge of his nose. Fuck, he had it bad.

GINGERSNAP

I'm fine. Interesting funeral. I don't think I've been to one with so many motorcycles.

With his cigarette resting between two fingers, he reached up, pinched a section of beard between his fingers and twisted, thinking of a response.

If she were a decent woman, she'd not want to be involved with him. If she were a *sane* woman, she wouldn't get involved with him once she knew the full extent, or to the extent one can know without a patch. That didn't mean he was ready to give her up.

PRK

> He was a loyal brother and deserved a proper sendoff. Sorry about ditching you, but thank you for coming.

Gah, he sounded like a goddamn tool. Since when did he apologize for that stuff, for club business and mean it? Sure, it was rude, but his club came first. He never felt bad for that.

It had been far too fucking long since he actually dated anyone. Not that they were dating. Were they dating? Shit, he wanted to date her.

GINGERSNAP

> Thank you for inviting me.

She was fucking perfect. All right, time to nut up. He had to stop acting like a fourteen-year-old with a boner next to his crush.

Putting his cigarette between his lips, he inhaled deeply. The burn of the nicotine and the smoke in his lungs reminded him of who he was—vice fucking president of Odin's Fury, Ohio Chapter. Closing his eyes, he exhaled out of his nostrils and enabled dragon mode.

PRK

> Your marks have to be fading. Can't have that. You up for another session soon?

GINGERSNAP

Absolutely.

Her response was quick, and he sat forward. Leaning his forearms on his spread thighs, he smiled at the phone. Gingersnap may have it as bad as he did. At least he had that going for him. A chick who was into him would forgive a lot of his awkward fuck ups.

PRK

Tomorrow. Dinner first.

A date. Yes. He wanted a proper date. Taking the cigarette between his fingers, he studied the cherry on the end. She was a proper lady, after all. She deserved dinner before he beat her ass. The thought of her ass, round, glowing bright red from his paddle had his cock stiffening in his pants. Gripping the crotch of his jeans, he shifted, trying to get comfortable.

GINGERSNAP

I have work. I won't be available until around 9.

That worked for him. He could handle club business during the day and play time at night. Pulling his cigarette from his mouth, he couldn't wipe the grin off his face if he'd tried. He'd been handed the ideal set up for a biker—a chick busy during the day, and free at night. Bonus points because she was kinky as fuck like him.

PRK

I'll pick you up at 9.

GINGERSNAP

On your bike?

Fuck. His bike? She wanted to ride on his bike. Of course she did. The thing was sexy as hell. He may be into her, but putting Gingersnap on the back of his bike sent a message he wasn't necessarily ready to send.

GINGERSNAP

> I just wanted to know how to dress. I imagine a skirt wouldn't be a good idea on a bike.

When her second message came in, he realized he may have taken too long to respond. Slipping his smoke back between his lips, he considered the idea of her in a skirt before he texted back.

PRK

> Nah, too cold to take the bike at night now. I'll get you in my truck.

Liar. He'd ride in the snow if he wanted to.

GINGERSNAP

> Okay. Sounds great.

He tried to chase the pang of guilt away with another drag of his cigarette.

PRK

> You got a name?

That had to be the clumsiest topic shift he'd ever done. He'd blame the bourbon. Craft beers were more his style. They came in a bunch of quirky flavors, and he liked quirks.

GINGERSNAP

> Liz. You?

More smiles. Liz. Envisioning her, the name fit. It made him think of Queen Elizabeth, and he thought she had red hair, like his Liz.

His?

He needed to pump the brakes on those types of thoughts. She wasn't his anything, nothing more than a woman he wanted to get to know and liked to hit. It didn't make Liz his.

PRK

Very regal.

He dodged the question about his own name. He wasn't sure he wanted to offer it. Though she did deserve something. Something beyond his scene name.

PRK

My friends call me Dash.

There. That would do. Besides, she'd seen his road name on his cut by now. She'd just been a classy bitch and not asked about it.

GINGERSNAP

We're friends now?

Ah. His playful—nothing. She wasn't his. He really needed to stop thinking shit like that.

PRK

We sure as shit ain't enemies.

GINGERSNAP

LOL. Fair point. Though, do you often hit your enemies?

PRK

Only the ones I really like.

"Someone's in a good mood."

Blue's voice was far too close, and it snapped Dash out of his goofy good mood. He'd been distracted flirting via text and hadn't been aware of his surroundings. He hadn't even heard the door open. The smile left his face. He had an image to maintain, afterall.

The still topless woman led Mooky to the patio section. Once he took a seat in an Adirondack chair, she slid into his lap and offered his club brother a joint, the only drug permitted on their club house property. She extended a hand toward Dash and flipped her fingers in a gesture meant to beckon something from him.

He gave her the lighter.

"So many morose motherfuckers in there," she commented as Mooky puffed the weed to life. "It's nice to see some smiles."

"Those guys are having a good time." Dash jerked a thumb toward the clubhouse. The men had pussy and booze. Most bikers viewed that as a perfect evening.

She shrugged as she snuggled into Mooky. "Not as good as you. If I didn't know any better, I'd say you were flirting."

Mooky chuckled as he passed her the joint.

Snuffing out his cigarette, Dash snorted. His phone vibrated, and he stuffed it in his pocket. He wasn't ready to share Liz with his club yet. Another realization he wasn't prepared for. He stood, nearly knocking the chair back. "I think I need another shot."

"Out of Wild Turkey." Mooky nipped at Blue's earlobe, using his free hands to fondle her breasts.

"Thank Christ." Dash scrubbed his face. "Tequila?"

"Always," Blue all but purred as she pulled the joint from her lips and exhaled.

He turned to leave. He suspected they'd fuck in front of him if he'd stayed. He wasn't in the mood to watch that, not when he had a text from Liz burning in his pocket. Plus, he wasn't that much of a voyeur, anyway.

Opening the back door to the clubhouse, Halestorm's *The Familiar Taste of Poison* filled his ears, and he smirked. If he were a superstitious man, he'd think it a sign. Amused, he headed for the bar to get some tequila.

CHAPTER 2

Gingersnap

"One, there are four outfits laid out on my bed. I've tried them on about fifty times. He'll be here in ten minutes," Liz dropped yet another shirt onto a pile of clothing she had rejected to wear that evening. "I haven't been on a date since, well…" She trailed off, not wanting to even mention him while talking to her friend on speaker phone and choosing an outfit.

No need to taint an evening that she truly expected to be fantastic. She lifted another blouse and sauntered over to her full length mirror to hold it up to herself.

"And definitely haven't been on a first date in years. Help me stop overthinking things." Shaking her head, she threw the top over her head and covered her face in frustration. She'd never get dressed at this rate.

Pacing in her bedroom, she wore a lacy teal bra and panty set she bought earlier that day specifically for that night. She snaked her fingers through her hair, ruffling it, thankful she hadn't done it yet.

She hadn't done her hair yet. Jesus, it was late enough and now her plan was to make him wait for her while she did her hair?

She'd always thought of herself as a low-maintenance woman. She prided herself in not requiring manicures, a metric ton of makeup, or a linen closet full of hair care products. Normally, she was confident enough to be herself. She couldn't figure out what it was about PRK—Dash that left her so insecure.

"First of all," Anemone began in an easy tone. "You need to breathe and remember that he's just a person. Remember that? People. And it's not like you haven't hung out with him before. One last thing."

Her voice picked up pitch and Liz could imagine her getting animated on the other end of the phone.

"You already had your first date—the coffee shop."

Stopping in her tracks, Liz blinked repeatedly. *They already had their first date?* "That wasn't a date."

"No?" Ane challenged in her gentle, yet stern way. "Two people alone, drinking coffee, listening to a bad acoustic cover of 90s soft rock. That's a date, sweetheart."

"No." Liz shook her head as though the unseen gesture would convince her friend of the denial. "We didn't meet up, it wasn't planned." She ticked her reasons off on her fingers, then paused. *What was she doing? Who, exactly, was she trying to convince? And why? Why did she need to convince anyone of anything?*

Ane let out an exaggerated sigh. "Okay, now you're just being sad. All I'm saying is that you're putting too much pressure on this thing. You two get along, you jive, and he's into you. Why are you stressing?"

Raking her fingers through her hair again, she turned to see herself in the mirror. *Listen to reason,* she told herself. Ane was right.

"You're a confident, successful, beautiful woman," Ane

pumped her up. "The only thing you *need* to worry about is if he is good enough for *you*."

Her doorbell rang. "Shit!" Startled by the unexpected noise, Liz bobbled her phone. Catching it, she held it in front of her face and spoke directly into it as though it were a walkie-talkie. "He's here. Gotta go. Love you, bye."

With a tap to the screen, she tossed her phone to the side, and wrapped her satin robe around herself.

Strong. Sexy. Confident. That was her plan.

Answering the door in her robe with her hair a tangled bun atop her head wasn't exactly what she'd intended. That wouldn't project that image at all. Too late, though. She had to embrace it.

Wearing only a few strokes of mascara and glossed lips, Liz opened the door. She leaned against the frame and offered him a sexy smile.

Black boots, dark wash jeans, and a simple dark button-down shirt which he wore untucked. The outside light reflected off his bald head. Had he combed his beard? The thought had her recalling the unexpected softness of the blond facial hair along her shoulder before he whispered dirty things into her ear and a slight chill of excitement rippled through her.

When her gaze met his, he gifted her with a lop-sided smile. "You are significantly under dressed."

Joining him in a slight chuckle, she suspected that her state of undress, while unexpected, was appreciated. If that didn't stroke her ego, she didn't know what would. She stepped back, opening the door wider to allow him entrance.

"I had some difficulty deciding what to wear," she admitted, using her sex kitten voice.

The generous and obvious once-over he gave her while entering the apartment did more than inflate her head. A flush swirled in her belly and crept up into her chest and continued to her cheeks.

Feeling bold, she ogled the way his jeans hugged the curves of his ass as he strode deeper into her apartment—through her living room and down the small hallway.

"Wait!" she called after him, closing the door. "Where are you going?"

"Helping," he hollered from down the hall.

*Helping? Surely he didn't mean to...*mortified that he'd not only see the disastrous state of her bedroom—it looked as though her closet had vomited on her bed and floor, but also by the idea he would be rifling through her personal things, Liz trotted after him.

He stood with his back to the door, his legs parted slightly, cupping his elbow with one hand, looking down at her bed and her outfit choices for the night. She walked up to him. He stroked his beard with a free hand, face pensive as he looked down at the selections.

"I just...I wasn't sure which look to go for." She tucked some of her barely combed hair behind her ear.

Hair.

She hadn't even gotten to style her hair yet. She'd wanted soft curls, like an effortlessly sexy look. They'd never leave her apartment at this rate. Self-consciously, she curled locks around her fingers.

"The one at the door was pretty hot. I'm not complaining, but it's not something I want to share with the world." He met her gaze and grinned. "Just yet."

Butterflies fluttered in her stomach and the heat in her cheeks betrayed her. Dodging his eyes, she tried to mask it by looking over the clothes. She'd picked out a teal cocktail dress, skinny jeans with a green blouse, and a floral top with a black flirty skirt.

"Something's missing." He shook his loose fist as he

turned, scanning her room. "These are all lovely." She smirked at the word coming from his lips. It seemed so out of character. "You'd rock every one of them." That sounded much more like the man she'd spoken to.

Getting down on his knees, he crouched near her bed.

"What... what are you doing?" she asked knowing full well what she hid under her bed. "I don't have any clothes under there."

From under her bed, he produced *the* box. With wide eyes, she stared at him. That box was sacred. How dare he invade her privacy, her space like that?

And why did it give her a thrill?

"That one." He pointed to the floral top with a black skirt while he rummaged through her toy box. "It's just missing something."

Bewildered, she reached for the clothes. Stepping into the skirt, she shimmied it up her hips. "I have some cute heels to go with it."

Dash reached into the box and then held up her butt plug in one hand and lube in the other.

With her top scrunched up over her breasts after she pulled it on, she stared at him. Her gaze darted between him and the plug he held in his hand. *He couldn't be serious.*

"I thought..." Her heart sank. "I thought we were going somewhere?" Cocking his head to the side, he peered at her. "We are, but we can't go anywhere if you aren't dressed." He wiggled the plug in his hand. "Completely."

Frozen by the surprise and confusion, she seemed to have lost her ability to do anything more than stare. His smile did nothing to ease her awkwardness, but it did cause her heart to trip over itself as it beat more rapidly. She felt her increased pulse between her thighs and squeezed them in anticipation for what his grin promised.

He stepped closer, closing the distance between them.

Switching to holding both items in one hand, he cocked his head to the side and studied her.

Her breath hitched.

With one hand now free, he used it to trail his fingertips along her exposed midriff. Goosebumps rose on her flesh. Her skin felt as though it lit on fire.

"Let me help you," he whispered before he brought his head down and nipped at her shoulder. The shirt slid down over her body, covering her, and she never wanted to be naked more in her life.

She closed her eyes as the feel of his warm mouth found the hollow of her throat. His teeth grazed her neck. A shudder rippled through her. Liz felt as though she were melting into a puddle at his touch.

"Turn around." His scorching breath danced along the shell of her ear.

Slowly, she spun, her back pressed against his front, the feel of stiffness rubbing against her ass.

Oh, now that was nice.

He brushed her hair aside and his beard lightly scratched against her neck. She moaned, pushing her ass into him.

"Bend."

With his hand on the small of her back, she did as instructed. Her palms rested on the mattress while he lifted the skirt she'd just put on. She looked over her shoulder. Dash got down on his knees.

Inhaling audibly, she closed her eyes. He trailed his fingers over her hips, taking her panties with them and sliding them down her thighs. His beard brushed her ass first, followed by the softness of his lips, finally his teeth. He pressed them into her flesh, and she groaned.

Kisses trailed downward until he slid his tongue along the crease where her ass met her thigh. More biting, and she shivered. Part of her wanted to laugh. The other half of her wanted to beg for more.

"Have you used this?" he asked after she heard a click.

"Huh?" It took her a minute to focus and connect to what he referenced. "The plug? Uh, no. It was a…oh."

He'd spread her ass cheeks and something cool and wet slid down her crease. "Wonderful."

She jumped at the feel of his fingers spreading over her tailbone area. Her heart rate picked up and she fisted the bedsheets. She'd been curious about butt stuff, but now to be actually faced with the prospect of something going up there, she wasn't so sure this was a good idea.

"Breathe," he coaxed and massaged her back slightly. "It will be much more enjoyable if you're relaxed."

Her heart raced with anticipation of the unknown—and the possible pain that came with it. "Breathe," he urged again.

Closing her eyes, she took a deep inhale, held it, and then let it out. Repeating it a few times, she released the bedding, and she felt the push.

With his fingers still spread over her, she assumed it was his thumb pressing against her back opening.

"Ahhh!" Her tight ring gave way and his digit slid up inside her.

"Keep breathing," he said.

The feeling of his finger, his wide thumb, dipping into her back door had her mind fogging. Her knees wobbled, and she locked her elbows so she wouldn't face plant on the bed.

"Oh dear god!" Her eyes snapped open at the feeling of his thumb twisting.

Taking in a sharp inhale, she jerked slightly. He ran a finger along her inner folds and didn't hesitate to find her clit. He rubbed against it, causing her to rock back and forth. The added stimulation of his thumb moving in and out of her intensified what he did to her pussy. The sensations were almost enough to short circuit her brain.

Her breathing shifted to shallow, short gasps as he worked his thumb in and out and in again. Her eyes rolled back into her head as he applied more pressure on her clit. Out went his thumb and in went something wider. Longer. She shuddered with the pinch to her clit as her ass filled.

"Oh God!"

Pop.

The plug was in and she trembled while the quake of an orgasm rippled through her.

CHAPTER 3

Dash

*D*ash had planned to take Liz to a cute Italian restaurant with low lighting and a romantic atmosphere. He'd wanted them to have a normal vanilla evening of getting to know one another. His intentions were pure. Drumming his fingers on the steering wheel of his truck, he bopped his head to the beat of *Black Betty* by Ram Jam, doing his best to hide the disappointment in himself. She'd deserved a better date—first date.

But she answered the door in that threadbare robe, wearing the hottest fucking bra and panty set he'd ever seen. He was just a man, and not a good one at that. His little vixen knew exactly what she'd done, and he was nothing if not accommodating with his partners. So, he'd come up with something on the fly.

And fly they did if he wanted to get any sort of food in her. The speed limits on these roads were merely a suggestion this time of night anyway, right?

Unfortunately, the time it took to get her prepped,

dressed, and for her to do whatever it was she did with her hair, meant that their choices for dinner dwindled. He wanted to take her somewhere nicer, but the Broken Spoke seemed their only option now.

Owned by the club, he knew he'd get no flack for wanting food this late. It also meant his brothers would be there. Pulling up to the Spoke in a cage, instead of his Road King, meant his brothers would notice.

Hell, they'd notice because Liz was a fucking hot redhead. It didn't matter what he drove to get there. Blondes were a dime a dozen, but fiery bitches—they were hard to come by. Add to it, he didn't have her on his bike—they'd think he wasn't serious about her. Was he?

Fuck him running. Normally, he prided himself on his ability to plan. He swerved to hit yet another pothole just to hear her groan as the plug shifted in her ass, and to prove to himself that yes, he did in fact plan shit. But he realized he may have made the wrong decision when it came to which vehicle he'd chosen. Taking her to the Spoke meant exposing her to the club.

Sure, she'd been at the funeral, but with all the people there, she was written off as just another citizen. Showing up at the Spoke *with him*—yeah, they'd notice. Not to mention, she'd notice the colors. They hadn't exactly spoken about his club involvement. He screwed himself for sure.

With his hand on her thigh, he felt the muscles in her leg tightening as she squeezed. It sparked a grin. The plug had worked. Since she wasn't all that experienced with ass play, he knew he'd have to get it out soon. Which was why he'd insisted on her bringing a large purse.

They pulled into the half-paved and half-gravel lot. He immediately counted the bikes and noted the prospect at the door. Romeo's and Mittens' bikes stood out against the rest.

Shouldn't his brothers be on their way home? Too late to turn back now.

"Sorry it's not a nicer place." He patted her leg. "Plans had to be adjusted." He grinned because he wasn't about to apologize for why they'd had to adjust plans. "Next time."

Her pale blue eyes rimmed with arousal from having hit every bump on the way there. Though, he suspected there was a post-orgasmic glow there as well. It looked good on her, and the half chub in his pants persisted.

"I'm sure it's fine." A sultry smile spread across her lips.

That did nothing to ease the strain in his jeans. Truly a minx, he'd never be convinced she didn't know exactly what she did to him.

He opened the door and got out of the truck. Pausing a moment, he took a deep inhale of the Ohio night before he reached back inside the cab. He grabbed his cut from the backseat and slammed the door. He trotted around to get to her side. He may be an asshole, but he still had some gentlemanly traits. After he opened the door, he extended his hand, and offered to help her down. Despite having chosen the smooth pavement out of habit—bikes didn't do well on gravel—she wobbled slightly once she jumped down from the cab. He grinned knowing full well it wasn't the heels she wore which made her knees weak. Though, heels would make navigating the gravel difficult as they crossed the rest of the lot on the way to the door.

Once out of the truck, he reached over her to place his cut on the roof. He gripped her hips and pressed her back against it.

Wide-eyed, she peered at him, but did nothing to fight his advances. She allowed him to guide her, and even softened her expression seconds after the surprise wore off. She graced him with a smirk and brought her hands over his shoulders before rolling her hips forward to graze against his half-mast erection.

Sliding his hands over her hips and around to her ass, he dug his fingers in, squeezing her pale ass beneath. She moaned the most beautiful sound, and it was all he could do not to bend her over and fuck her in the parking lot.

Dipping his head down, he pressed his lips over hers. Liz pulled him hard against her body as he wedged his leg between her thighs. He massaged her ass.

She groaned into their kiss.

Sweat beaded on his back beneath his shirt. His cock stiffened beneath his jeans and threatened to punch a hole through his zipper. His gentle caresses of her butt grew firmer, harder, to the point he might leave little fingerprint bruises. The idea only drove him to press harder into her—then she whimpered and his knees all but buckled.

This woman would be his undoing.

He'd promised her a date. He'd wanted it to be vanilla. That shit went out the window, but he still promised her a date. Fucking her in the parking lot was not a date.

Dinner, asshole. Feed her. Reign it the fuck in.

Nipping at her lip, he slowly pulled his mouth away. His hands lingered in place before he relented in the pressure he'd applied. Trying to catch his breath, he hung his head, counted to three, then brought himself back in. Though instead of kissing, because if he did that, he'd never get her out of the parking lot, he did the next best thing. Pressing his forehead against hers, he fought the urge to use a cliché line. "You have no business being this fucking hot."

She laughed. "I'll work on that."

He spun her, still laughing, to press her front to the truck. With a yank of her hips, she bent slightly, the moan caught in her throat through the laugh. That wouldn't do.

Three quick swats to each ass cheek with his open palm

were muffled by the skirt. She yelped each time and squirmed. Running his right hand up the back of her neck, he grabbed a fistful of her hair. He'd insisted she wear it loose for this very reason, he loved her hair. He could run his fingers through it for hours if given the opportunity—so soft, so silky—so not where his head needed to be right then. *Focus.* He pulled her head back, forcing her to arch her neck. The long line begged to be teased. His mouth watered with the idea of nipping and sucking her jawline then down.

"I adore your snarky attitude," he whispered in her ear as she wiggled against his body. He'd effectively pinned her between himself and the truck so her movements were limited to grinding that sweet ass against his very stiff cock.

Like hell she didn't know what she did to him.

"Thank you, sir."

The husky response had his dick twitching in his pants. She added 'sir.' She'd already obliterated his will for a vanilla evening. There was no use in keeping to that now.

With a nip to her neck, he stepped back. He grabbed his cut from the top of the truck and shrugged it on. He couldn't go to the Spoke without his colors. Taking her wrist, he gently turned her. The look in her slightly hooded eyes sealed the deal.

"Fuck it." His hand slid down and took hers, interlocking their fingers as he led her across the lot toward the entrance of the Broken Spoke.

The plug had to come out, anyway. He'd been lying to himself this whole night if he thought they were capable of a vanilla evening.

The gratuitous once over from the prospect, who worked as a bouncer at the door of the bar, earned him a glare of warning from Dash. His woman. His internal dragon voiced his possessiveness.

Once inside, he weaved her through the busy bar. He kept

his head down, not needing any diversions right now. She tugged back when he put his hand on the women's bathroom door.

"Wait!" she called over the sound of the tail end of *Hey Joe* by Hendrix. "What are you—"

No time. He aimed for spontaneity and keeping her off kilter. She offered no further resistance when he entered the bathroom with her in tow. Dropping her hand, he surveyed the bathroom. He whistled once inside and the two women standing at the mirror eyed him as though he'd invaded the inner sanctum.

"Out." His voice rumbled with the feral desire he needed to quench.

Still giving wary looks, the two women in the bathroom rushed out. Dash locked the door behind them. Shifting focus to his conquest, he grinned.

He couldn't read the look on her face. He suspected it was somewhere between anxious and excited. He hoped she leaned more toward the latter of the two.

"Face the mirrors, bend over a little bit, and put your hands on the counter," he ordered in a tone that left no room for argument. "Our safe words are still in play." He wasn't about to do anything without her permission. "If any of this is too much for you, what is your safe word to stop everything?"

"Red," she whispered immediately, but didn't move.

"What color are we, Liz?" he asked, watching her features.

She pressed teeth into her bottom lip as she met his gaze. There was a good foot or two between them. He purposely did not want to invade her space. She may have a plug in her ass. It may have her feeling slightly more submissive than normal. It needed to be her choice to play —and that choice needed to be made with a clear—well clearish head.

"Green." Her cheeks turned the most adorable shade of red he'd ever seen.

Nodding, he grinned his approval and waited for her to obey his order.

The closed door to the bathroom muffled the soft rock music coming from the speakers and the conversation from the crowd at the bar. It allowed him to focus more fully on her, to take note of her body's tension.

Slowly, she turned and gazed at him in the mirror. Her slightly shaking hands rested on the counter and she bent timidly. The view was delightful, but could be better. Stepping behind her, he gently kicked at her feet.

Following his non-verbal command, she shuffled her legs apart, making sure to keep an eye on him. He nodded, offering approval, but when she stopped, it wasn't enough. So he tapped her thighs, coaxing more. He heard the gulp, saw the blush, but he had to hand it to her. She kept her eye on him as she further parted her legs.

To some, it might have been obscene. To him, it was fucking glorious the way she spread for him—just for him. He didn't need drugs—this was his high.

"Do you have experience playing in public?" He ran his hands up and down her back and massaged her shoulders a bit to try to ease the tension. She needed to relax a bit more for this to be enjoyable. That was his goal, to make sure they both enjoyed playtime.

"A little," she whispered.

"Outside of play spaces?" He assumed since she went to events meant for play, she'd have to have played there. This was different, far different.

When he brought his hands down to her ass, digging his fingers in, squeezing the cheeks together, and then pulling them apart slightly, she gasped and bit down on her lip. That sound, oh that sound was his favorite sound in the world.

She moaned as her lids fluttered closed. Okay, it was a tie, moan or groan—any noises from her were his favorite. Either way he had learned a valuable lesson. Her ass was quite the erogenous zone.

"N-no." Her husky stammer was laced with need.

"It's exciting, isn't it?" He flipped her skirt up.

"Yes," she hissed and pushed back against his hands.

Chuckling, he gave her a slap to each cheek. "Stay still."

A demand he knew would be unmanageable. It didn't mean he couldn't enjoy her struggle with compliance.

Whining, she let her head fall. "Yes, sir."

Dash trailed his finger down her panty-covered ass crack, pressing the plug so it entered her deeper. She groaned, rocking up on the balls of her feet. His smug grin reflected his enjoyment at being able to exploit the impossible standard he'd placed on her.

Another quick set of slaps, one for each side. She gasped with each impact. His hand dipped lower between her legs, and found her pussy soaked. Rubbing his fingers through her lace covered slit, he snickered. "Do I need to remind you that panties are a privilege denied to many?"

"No, sir," she whimpered as her hips rocked of their own accord.

He found her clit and applied pressure with one hand, while the other pushed the plug again. "Are you wearing them responsibly?"

She arched her back and groaned while he varied the pressure with each hand. "No, sir."

"I'm going to take them from you." He took his hands away.

Her continued whimpers delighted him and made his cock strain that much more against his zipper while he tugged down the lacy panties. He tapped one foot and then the other to get her to step out of them. Pocketing the bit of fabric, he admired what he had before him. "Much better." He returned to stroking her pussy with one hand and taking the base of the plug with the other. He wanted her thoroughly aroused when he pulled it from her. The experience was far better when on the verge of orgasm.

Her breathing increased, and then hitched as she pushed back against his hands again. It was time. As gently as he could, he pulled the plug back until her anal ring gave way, and it popped the widest portion from her opening.

Her yelp called to the deepest parts of his dominant nature. It was all he could do not to slam his cock home in her ass. Restraint. He needed to do it properly.

"What color are we?" he asked, praying to all that was holy she wasn't going to use a safe word on him.

"Green," she panted, and he thanked all the deities he could think of while he pumped the plug in and out of her virginal asshole.

Her legs shook and her whines mixed with grunts. She was close. He could feel it in the wetness of her pussy and the way she wriggled, eager for more. He was eager too, but it would require taking his hands from her. Choosing to keep the plug buried, but not seated inside her, he used the hand he'd been teasing her sensitive folds with to fish the condom from the inside pocket of his cut and put it between his teeth.

Undoing the button, then the fly of his jeans, the cool air greeted his thighs and painfully erect cock when his pants dropped. She continued to moan and push back on the plug as he ripped the wrapper of the condom open.

"I'm going to fuck you, Liz," he told her in no uncertain terms. "I'm going to fuck your ass hard and you're going to love it." He wanted to give her time to safe word, as much as he didn't want to hear it. He needed to offer her time to stop him.

Her body stiffened slightly, but she kept moving back

onto the plug. Dash grinned at the nervousness while sheathing his cock with the green condom. From his jeans pocket, he pulled the lube he'd borrowed from her apartment. Using his thumb, he flicked the cap open. Doing it all one handed was a testament to his dexterity.

A generous glob of lube plopped onto his shaft. He leaned over her body, purposely shoving the plug all the way in again, popping it in place, causing her to groan loudly, and put the bottle of lube down while his free hand stroked his cock to coat it in slick gel.

"Just think how much deeper my cock will be," he taunted before he nipped her ear. "Thicker too. You can handle it though."

He righted himself, took a step back, and admired her ass. There were a million and nine things he wanted to do to that ass, but right now, fucking it was highest on the list. Taking his hand away from his dick, he dipped it between her legs to pinch at her swollen folds.

"Please," she begged, causing a feral growl to bubble up from his chest.

"What do you want?" he teased. He purposely avoided direct contact with her clit. Instead, he barely grazed it— offering enough to keep her aroused but not enough to send her over the edge.

"More, please, just more. I'm close," she trembled and slapped her hand against the bathroom counter.

"I want you to come with my cock in your ass. You'll do it for me, won't you?" He pulled the plug from her again. It gave easier this time—ah—just what he wanted to see. She was warmed up—her body was ready.

"Please," she begged again.

This woman would absolutely destroy him. Dropping the plug on the floor, he used his now empty hand to pump his dick. He slid two fingers into her anus, and they entered her without much resistance. All signs pointed toward "go."

"Do you feel that?" he asked as she bucked. His thumb dipped into her pussy and her walls spasmed around it.

"Yes," she hissed.

"It's just my fingers, but you're begging me. It's making it hard to hold back."

"Please!" she screamed as her fist slammed against the counter. Her chest, flushed with her need, heaved. Her reflection silently pled with him to send her over the edge.

Jesus Christ.

Sliding his fingers from her ass and her pussy, he positioned his cock at the entrance. "I need you to breathe deep."

She had to relax, she had to be calm. It'd hurt far more than it should if she tensed.

On her inhale, he pushed the rounded tip of his cock against the tight opening and pressed harder on her clit.

"Let it out," he urged.

When she did, he flexed his hips. Her well-worked ring gave, and welcomed him into her hot backdoor. Slowly, he slid every inch of himself up inside her, feeling her body stiffen. Her hole flexed around him, almost milking his cock.

She squealed, taking him. He focused his fingers on her clit—alternating between the amount of pressure while stroking her. His entire body felt ablaze, and he controlled his own breathing in an attempt not to blow on the first thrust. She was goddamn tight.

Once fully seated inside her, he let her get accustomed to him. His head fell back and his hands rested on her hips. *In through the nose and out through the mouth.* He had to remind himself how to breathe. *Focus.* This woman tested every bit of his self-control. She summoned his dominant side and then brought him to his knees with her responsiveness.

The heat around his dick, the pulsing pressure, the way

she squirmed against him while panting, trying to catch her breath. Jesus-fucking-Christ, did she just shiver? He swallowed hard. This was Valhalla. He found it. Gingersnap—Liz was it.

Now he needed to bring her to the same headspace he was in. He needed to be as deep in her submission as he was in his dominance.

"I'm inside you," he taunted.

"Oh god," she groaned.

"You're tight as fuck," he added, stroking her slit. "So fucking tight."

To his surprise, her hips rolled far sooner than he'd expected.

"Please," she gritted. "Please fuck me. I need it."

He pulled back, not taking his cock entirely out. Leaving the thick head inside her, he slammed home, shoving her against the counter. Her loud grunt timed perfectly with the spasm around his cock.

"Fuck." He pinched her clit. Deciding his brain may have blown a gasket, his vocabulary had diminished significantly.

For her sake, despite how much he wanted to pound into her, he held back and gave her long deep strokes. She wriggled under him, making feral noises each time he pinched or stroked her clit on the inward motion.

His balls tightened and he tried to hold off. Her orgasm was far more important than his own, but he wasn't sure how much longer he could prevent it. Using his free hand, he gripped her shoulder, pulling her back on him for a particularly deep thrust.

She was close. He could feel how close she was. His hand was soaked, and from the way her asshole kept tightening around him, he knew it wouldn't be much longer. Gritting his teeth, he pulled back and slammed in one more time. She screamed and her hole clamped down around him, pulsing, effectively milking him.

His thrusts were far shorter. The smooth movements turned into uncoordinated jerks as his muscles strained. His calf muscles threatened to snap, but he needed to keep going for her. Somewhere between pain and rocketing to the moon he exploded. As he followed her over the edge, he erupted while rubbing her pussy through her own release. His orgasm pulsed deep within her, filling his condom. Collapsing over her back, he took a moment to catch his breath while pushing her hair aside and kissing the back of her neck.

CHAPTER 4

Gingersnap

*I*f Dash wasn't buried inside her, pinning her against the counter, she doubted her legs would hold her. When he withdrew, she couldn't help but groan as the empty, loose feeling in her rear took over her awareness. Liz had somehow forgotten where they were in the fog of her submission. It had felt amazing. Never in her life had she thought anal sex could be so enjoyable.

When muffled voices came to her awareness, she turned her head toward the door as people knocked and another voice mentioned something about cleaning. Dash held her hips and spun her slowly. Facing him, she focused on his features, his flushed face, and the sweat beading on his bald head.

He grinned, stroking her hair. "Fucking amazing," he whispered before kissing her forehead. "You okay?"

Nodding, she tried to move away. Using his arms, he caged her in, keeping her against the counter.

"I need. I need to go." Her brain just couldn't seem to

connect with words, but the urge to use the restroom taunted her.

"In a minute," he said between soft kisses. "Let's come back to Earth first, okay?"

Swallowing, her mouth felt like the Sahara. "Okay."

Resting her head on his shoulder wasn't as easy as she wanted it to be. He shifted, bending down, and then the thud of something hitting the sink drew her attention. The water ran, and he splashed something. "In your purse there is a gallon zip-lock bag. I'm going to get it, okay?"

Wrapping her arms around him, she nuzzled into his neck, smelling the leather, the scent of his body wash, or deodorant, and the lingering cigarette smell. He smoked, she remembered that now.

"Okay," she whispered into his neck.

With one arm around her waist, holding her against him, he shifted about. As she came back to the present, more around her registered. The muffled music on the other side of the door reminded her they were in public. The sound of a zip-lock bag opening and then snapping shut had her curious.

"What are you doing?"

He chuckled. "Well, it's wet. I don't want it to ruin what you have in this nice purse, and I want to use it again at a later date, so this is the only way I could think to keep it."

She furrowed her brows. "What?" *What was he talking about?* "What do you want to use?"

Her eyes closed at the feeling of his nose nuzzling into her neck, and his beard along her shoulder. She shuddered, her skin still sensitive from post-orgasmic bliss.

"The plug. I'm going to fuck your ass again, and it will need to be prepped." He growled in her ear before nipping at her earlobe.

Her pussy twitched, her stomach fluttered, and she moaned in anticipation. "Not here."

He laughed heartily, shaking both of them with the motion. "No, baby. Even if I wanted to, I do need recovery time." He kissed her temple and stepped back, still holding her hips. "Can you stand?"

"Yeah," she responded as though it was a ludicrous question. Of course she could stand. At least, she wanted to believe that.

Tentatively, he pulled his hands away. The feeling of his gaze locked on her felt both comforting and intimidating in the most erotic of ways. Thankfully, her knees had remembered how to work and she didn't topple to the floor. She no longer felt like a newborn fawn.

Taking a few steps, she headed toward the bathroom stall. "I need to..."

She couldn't finish the sentence.

Nodding, he went to the door. "I'll leave you to it. But I won't be far. I'll be on the other side. I'll make sure the kitchen stays open. I don't know about you, but after that, I'm fucking starved."

Grateful he had no intention of remaining in the bathroom while she cleaned herself up, she smiled at him. "Okay."

Watching him unlock and open the door, the soft rock playing on the other side of the door grew louder. She took that opportunity to duck into a stall and sat down to take care of business.

Panties. Shit. He didn't give her back her panties. Her bag was on the counter. *Fuck.* If he had put them in there, she would have had no access to them. Running her hands over her face, she took a deep breath. Well, looks like she would be panty-free for a little bit.

"I'm telling you, some shady shit went on in here." A female voice on the other side of the bathroom stall

33

announced. Liz realized she wasn't alone in the bathroom anymore.

"You always think shady shit is going on. They said it needed to be cleaned," another woman offered.

"Yeah, but prospects clean the bathrooms, not vice presidents," the first woman countered.

Vice President?

Dash was vice president of what? While she had come out of the post-orgasm fog of submission somewhat, her mind still wasn't fully clear. She'd been in sub-space before, but the session with Dash left her in a deeper state than she'd ever been. It'd been damn near trance-like. Her brain had literally shut off and all she could do was experience the overwhelming pleasure.

Sitting on the toilet, she covered her face with her hands and focused on her breathing while she relived the experience in her mind. She had some time. She wanted to wait for the two women to leave the bathroom before exiting the stall.

———

ONCE SHE LEFT THE BATHROOM, hands clean but still feeling loose, though not so slippery, Liz found Dash waiting at the door. Smiling, she tucked a lock of hair behind her ear. She dipped her chin as her cheeks heated with a flush. The second wave of arousal hit her when she thought of how he'd just taken her in the bathroom.

"You good?" he asked over the sound of the Rolling Stones playing on the speakers.

"Yeah." She stepped closer. The scent of his freshly smoked cigarette practically slapped her in the face, but she pushed it aside. There were more pressing matters. "I'm missing something."

A cocky half smile spread on his face as he wrapped an arm around her waist. "Oh? What is that?" He led her deeper into the bar. "Your anal virginity?"

Her stomach fluttered.

"Ass." She laughed nervously and slapped his shoulder.

"Yes, it's quite nice." He chuckled with her.

"Oh my god!" She brought her hands up and covered her face in exasperation, scrubbing for a second and then dropping them. "I meant my panties."

She hadn't realized she said it so loud. The snorts and looks from those around her only added to the embarrassment.

He laughed harder and pulled her closer. "I told you they were a privilege," he whispered in her ear. "You lost that privilege."

Her mouth fell open. He couldn't be serious. She was in a skirt, in public, and this was not a play space. This was real life. Her gaze darted around, and for a second she felt like everyone around them knew. They knew what she and Dash had done, and they knew now she was panty-less.

"Hey." Dash cupped her face with his hands. "Hey. Come back."

The tender tone starkly contrasted his deeper, dominant one, and the butterflies in her heart fluttered far too emphatically for her liking.

If her mouth hadn't been so dry, she would have swallowed down her panic. Scanning his gray eyes for answers, she couldn't find words. He couldn't be serious.

"This is public play," he reminded her and rested his forehead on hers. "You said you were into this."

"I never," she started. "I never—this isn't what—" This wasn't what she had meant. She'd meant play parties. She'd meant kink events. This was a completely different sort of head trip.

He nodded, bringing her focus back to him. He dipped down and placed a gentle kiss on her lips. With his arms wrapped around her, his affections disarmed her almost as much as the tone he'd used to get her attention.

Once he broke the kiss, he met her gaze. "Tell me your color."

Color? He wanted a color. Shit. They were still playing. The stop-light system still applied. *Her color. What was her color?*

"Yellow." She was still turned on as all get out, but conflicted about being panty-less in public. This wasn't a designated play place.

He grinned. "Good. We still have some dinner to eat."

"Can I get a drink?" she asked.

"This is a bar." He snickered. "Of course."

CHAPTER 5

Dash

*O*nce Dash got some food and a bottle of water in her, Liz relaxed. She was definitely out of the sub-space fog and over the anxiety of being out in public without panties. Her ass was far too fantastic to ever be covered by any sort of cloth, no matter how skimpy. Now that he'd had it, he'd want it again, and panties would limit his access. So, her panty privileges were now permanently revoked. He'd tell her eventually, but not right now. Nah, now they were talking about her and how she'd gotten into nursing.

Munching on French fries and sipping craft beer, he listened to her. She was truly an amazing, selfless woman. How she hadn't been snatched up by a decent guy was beyond him, but that wasn't his problem. Nope. Now that he had her, he wouldn't give her up so easily. He'd gladly reap the benefits of everyone else's oversight.

"So…" She leaned over the table, moved her half-eaten burger to the side, and rested on her elbows with her hands clasped together.

"So." He mimicked her posture and met her beautiful light blue gaze.

"Rumor has it you are a vice president," she said with an arched brow.

He chuckled and leaned back, taking a large swallow of his beer. "Acting. Acting vice president."

"Of?" she asked, raising her brows expectantly.

Furrowing his own brows, he peered at her. Glancing around, the biker presence was undeniable. Most of the cuts here were Odin's Fury. They were the only 1% hanging around tonight. The rest of the cuts were citizens who had riding clubs. They were law-abiding and normal clubs. Similar to his own club in that they rode motorcycles—usually Harleys, but nothing like his at all—in that they weren't criminals to put it bluntly.

Not every man who wore a cut and rode a motorcycle had what it took to be a one percenter. In 1947, after the Hollister riot, the American Motorcyclist Association made the distinction. Ninety-nine percent of motorcyclists were law-abiding. Dash, his brothers, and the men like him proudly wore their diamond one percent patch proclaiming their outlaw status.

He earned that patch. He bled for that patch. He sacrificed for it. He killed for it. It was his proudest achievement.

When he met her eyes, he grinned. "Well, I'm not one for suits or nine-to-five, so I thought it was obvious. I'm the acting VP of Odin's Fury MC, Ohio Chapter."

Recognition dawned in her eyes and then her cheeks turned that cute shade of pink when she became embarrassed. He loved that look on her.

"Oh." As her own gaze panned the other patrons, he had no doubt she took notice of the other cuts, and the other members. "What does that mean?"

Taking a deep breath, he pretended to search for the

French fry that most resembled a cigarette. He could really use one right then. He supposed this conversation was a long time coming. He was surprised it hadn't happened yet. She'd seen his cut, she'd attended the funeral, hell, she should have asked about this a lot sooner.

"It means I'm second in command for my club." He surveyed her expression for a response to his intentionally vague answer. She was a good woman. His lifestyle wasn't for her, he knew that, but he was far too selfish to let that stop him from seeing her. He'd gone down the damn rabbit hole. He'd sampled the forbidden fruit. He'd tasted pure bliss and he'd be an asshole to walk away now.

Her silence and blank expression were enough to tell him that what he said meant nothing to her. Dash wasn't sure how he wanted to explain this. Shit. He didn't *want* to explain it. This was definitely a drawback to getting involved with someone he didn't meet at the clubhouse. Sure, club whores had their baggage and were just in it for the thrill, but at least they knew the deal.

The daughters of bikers tended to be fucking nuts and he wouldn't get caught sticking his dick in a bear trap like that. Plus, that meant dealing with her daddy, most of the time. *No, thank you.*

So, here he was. He had to try to explain his lifestyle to her without scaring her off. "We're a bunch of guys who like riding. We are enthusiasts for American made bikes, mostly Harleys. We do charity work, we party, and we ride together. We also have a few businesses we run together. It's just a club."

Liz sipped at a bottle of beer as she canted her head to the side and listened. He watched her intently for signs of alarm, something telling him that he'd said the wrong thing. She gave him nothing. Her silence made Nickelback's *Burn it to the Ground* louder in his ears. She needed to give him something.

"There was a show on TV about bikers," she said.

Dash wasn't sure whether to be thankful or question her because that sounded like she hadn't watched it.

"Yes," he said through a laugh. "But that was over-dramatized for good TV. We're just a bunch of guys, mostly veterans, who just hang out and like booze and parties."

She nodded. "I'll have to watch it."

"You'll just get scared," he warned. "It's exaggerated."

She arched a brow at him. "You sound like you don't want me to." A wicked grin grew on her face. "That just makes me want to do it more."

Of course it did. Liz wasn't what he would call a brat. She was playful. If he really didn't want her to watch it, he could forbid it. Deep down, she was obedient. He hadn't a doubt in his mind that if he forbade it, she would obey. But that wasn't the type of dynamic they'd agreed to, and if he were to set a limit like that it'd be a gross misuse of her trust in him. So, nope. He wouldn't do that—no matter how much it would benefit him.

"How about this?" He leaned over the table. "We'll watch it together, and I'll call out the bullshit."

She twirled the beer in such a way the opening circled her lip and her tongue teased the mouth of the bottle. Dash shifted in his seat because, while he didn't think she did it purposely, it gave him a semi chub thinking about her lips doing the same thing to his dick.

Eventually, she took a sip of her beer. "Deal. I'll consider it research."

He couldn't help but laugh. *Research? Sure.* Let her call it what she wanted. At least if they watched it together, he could do some damage control and possibly limit her jumping to conclusions.

"Okay. So, then, in the name of research," he began as an idea came to him. "Why don't I take you back to the clubhouse so we can start tonight?"

The brothers had seen them together. There was no hiding her at this point. Once he took her to the clubhouse, he could at least let them all know she was off limits. She'd be around. He'd made that decision already. He couldn't quit her. So, he might as well make it so no one else touched his woman.

"All right."

"Good, I have plans for your ass. I'm not done with it yet."

CHAPTER 6

Gingersnap
Two Weeks Later

To say the first night she'd spent with Dash at the clubhouse had been jarring was an understatement. It'd reminded her of a frat house, but filled with grown ass hairy men in leather. At first, she'd felt too old to be there, and far too clothed, despite his no-panty rule. Women ran around topless or outright naked. Liquor flowed, and music played from speakers somewhere. When he'd told her it was a party, she hadn't really grasped it until she saw it.

Now that they spent almost every night together, they split their time between her apartment and his bedroom at the clubhouse. He didn't have a place of his own because he planned on going back to Montana.

He was from Montana.

She had to remind herself of that every so often. He didn't know when he'd be going back. That seemed to be the part she clung to, because it gave her an excuse to forget the rest.

He'd explained he was essentially on loan while the Ohio

chapter decided who their new vice president would be. She tried to ignore that there was an expiration date on their budding romance.

After watching a few episodes of *Sons of Anarchy*, she sort of understood. He insisted they weren't like that, and he didn't seem the type. Sure, he had a sadistic side, enjoyed bruising her ass, legs, or breasts, but he also had a soft side. The aftercare he gave her always left her feeling safe. He didn't remind her of the characters she watched in the show. He was far too real. They were, as he said, exaggerated.

The past few weeks had left her floating on air. When she was in Dash's orbit, she felt intoxicated by his dominance. Even when he wasn't actively playing, he was who he was, and she couldn't get enough of it. Even now, sliding her bra over her freshly striped breasts from the caning that morning had her slipping into a naturally submissive state. Their session ended two hours ago and, like the addict he'd apparently made her, she wanted another hit—literally. She'd take a bare ass spanking, a flogging, or a paddling. Anything.

She exited the bathroom wearing only a green lace demi-bra—she'd gotten used to the no panty rule and found herself not wearing them even when he wasn't around. Swiveling her hips as she walked she hoped to entice him before she had to go home and get ready for work.

"Got it." He sat, back facing her, on the edge of the queen-sized bed with a phone to his ear.

She rounded him and knelt between his widely spread legs. Resting her cheek on his inner thigh, she nuzzled when his hand raked through her hair.

"How long?" he asked the other person on the phone.

His expression hardened while he stared at the wood-paneled wall. Something, or someone, on the other side of the phone had put him in a dark mood.

Liz could fix that. Inching closer, she lifted the bit of

sheet he had covering his crotch. Grinning, she discovered his flaccid dick. She could definitely improve his mood. This was her specialty—she'd learned exactly how he liked certain things.

Without using her hands, she took the tip of him in her mouth. Swirling her tongue around and around, he twitched in her mouth. Before she could really get into it, his hand came to her shoulder and he gently moved her off him.

She peered up at him with a pleading expression, including a pout. Sure, they'd had sex a few hours ago, but his recovery time had already passed. With his thick calloused fingers, he stroked her jawline and shook his head.

She put her head back on his thigh, and he resumed running fingers through her hair. The affectionate and intimate gesture didn't abate her confusion. *Since when didn't he want a blow job? When did any man turn down a blow job?* Frowning, she traced a circle on his other thigh. His leg twitched. He lowered his hand over hers to stop the motion.

"Fuck," he growled into the phone and she pulled back.

Okay, something was really wrong and it sucked the sexy right out of the room. Sitting on her heels, she watched as he pushed off the bed and paced.

His free hand scrubbed through his beard, gripping it at the end as he nodded. "I have to bring this to church. You have to lay low, brother."

"We're coming. Keep your head down." He ended the call and turned to her.

The fire in his eyes was not the feral, dominant glow she was accustomed to seeing. His forehead creased and his mouth tightened into a thin line between his trimmed mustache and beard. For the first time since she'd met him, she was uncomfortable in the wrong way.

"Everything okay?" The obvious question was the only one that came to her mind.

"Club business," he said through clenched teeth. "We have to cut it short." He stalked toward her, stopping only when he stood over her with mere inches between them.

The position forced her neck to strain as she tilted her head upward to take in his features. He cupped the back of her head, entangling his fingers in her hair as he stared down at her still kneeling at the side of his bed.

"Anything I can do?" she asked.

With a heavy sigh, he gripped her hair tighter and closed his eyes. The tug of his hold on her hair caused a flutter in her sex. Her body didn't know about the mood of the room. All her body knew was that she was on her knees, and he had her hair. She liked that, but now wasn't the time. Especially, since he was silent as he held her like that for what had to be a full minute—or an eternity. They were the same, right?

When he released her, he stepped back. "I need to focus, and you need to stop being the sexy distraction that you are."

Frowning, she watched him. "I'm a distraction?" *What did that mean?*

He walked to the dresser, opened the middle drawer, and pulled out a pair of jeans. He stepped into them, before turning to face her. "I want nothing more than to keep playing, but I have shit to do and you have to go to work."

She pushed off the floor and stood. Feeling rejected and irrational, the impulse to cover her body, to somehow defend herself against her vulnerability surged. "I didn't, I don't—" she stammered, unsure what she wanted to say.

Once his zipper was up, and his button buttoned, he stalked toward her and took hold of her chin again. "You're being you. But right now, I can't. Something important just came up. I have to cut it short. My club comes first." He ran his thumb along her cheek.

She nodded before stepping into him and wrapping her

arms around his middle. He returned the hug and squeezed her. After a few seconds, he kissed the crown of her head.

Closing her eyes, she inhaled and smelled his morning cigarette. He'd gone down while she was in the bathroom. Apparently, they didn't smoke in the clubhouse.

The beginnings of sub-drop crept into her awareness. Her irrational neediness was a clear sign, and she needed to shut it down. Pulling away, she kept her head down while tucking hair behind her ear.

"Okay." The answer to her dropping was reassurance, but she couldn't ask that of him when he had something to do.

The two of them finished dressing in silence. The drop taunted her—twisted things—made her hyper-aware of any minor thing he did differently than he would normally. The fact that he hadn't helped her with her clothes, or fondled her through the process definitely meant something was up on his end. Her droopy-mind drifted toward rejection. Without clarity from him, not that she asked, her thoughts jumped to assumptions. The biggest one was that he'd been called home.

The highs of good submission carried the threat of the lows of sub-drop without aftercare. Were her logical brain functioning, she'd be able to combat the negative thoughts, but her drop robbed her of it. It nagged her, getting louder, repeating all her insecurities, drowning out reason.

As he walked her to her car in the early light of the morning, she became more convinced of it. At the car, he didn't pin her. He didn't prolong their time together. Instead, after she'd unlocked the door, he gave her a chaste kiss. Then he opened the door for her. She slid into her seat and peered up at him hoping—silently pleading for him to do something.

She needed one thing, just one gesture, tell her to lotion, something. If he did that she would know things were okay. If he just gave her a sign, she could shut the drop up.

"Drive safe, okay?" He closed the door.

She nodded and started the car, feeling numb.

He didn't. He didn't say it.

With a tap to her hood, he turned to walk back into the large cinder block building. Tears welled in her eyes as she put the car into gear. On some level, she knew she was over-reacting. However, she couldn't stop the emotions from bubbling up. When she pulled out of the parking lot, she had convinced herself this was the last time she'd see him.

CHAPTER 7

Dash

*L*iz looked far too haunted when Dash put her in the car. He didn't have time to deal with that right now. His club came first—the issue was far more pressing. She was physically safe. The same couldn't be said of his club. His woman would have to come later now that he'd gotten her out of harm's way.

Passing one of the more seasoned prospects as he stomped through the clubhouse, Dash caught his attention. "I'm gonna text you an address," he said as he pulled his burner from the pocket of his cut. "Watch over it. Anyone in or out, you let me know." His soon-to-be brother nodded. "The only one supposed to be there is a redhead."

Dash slapped him on the shoulder and gave a nod, sending him out the door. He fired off the text and continued on his way. The conflicting priorities grated against his mind as he climbed the stairs, two at a time, to get to Clark's room.

Fuck. He should be with Liz, but this shit needed to be

fucking dealt with. Sending the prospect to handle it felt wrong, but he did what he had to do.

Loyalty. Brotherhood. Sacrifices. That was what he'd signed up for. He knew this when he agreed to prospect. He knew this when he accepted his rockers. He knew it when he sewed that diamond patch on his cut. Agreeing to fill in as the VP only upped the ante.

God-mother-fucking-damnit. When he took on the role in the kink community, and called himself a dominant, he accepted responsibilities there too. He doubled down on that shit by getting involved with Liz.

As a dominant—her dominant—Dash knew she needed him. He had an obligation to her, a duty, and he'd failed in that. And wasn't that the most bitter fucking pill he'd ever swallowed. This was why relationships and club life may not be in the cards for him. A full-time power exchange dynamic was a commitment—they needed more than he could realistically provide. Play partners, no strings, no commitment. That's what he needed to stick to.

Whiskey was still missing in action. His club brother, a loyal man who put himself in harm's way for the benefit of the club, had been in contact, but they never were able to actually nail down where the hell he was located. They had precious little to go on, but they needed to get him the fuck back. Now.

Lifting his fist, he slammed it against Clark's door. "Prez! Gotta call church."

Clark yanked the door open. Dash got an eye full of naked as the day he was born, club president with a fist in his eye, rubbing sleep from it. "What the fuck?"

"Whiskey called. Need to update the brothers."

Dropping his hand from his face, the president of the Ohio Chapter of Odin's Fury Motorcycle Club eyed the acting Vice President and sobered. "Round 'em up. Church in an hour."

An hour. Reasonable. He'd even be able to fit in breakfast and a smoke while he waited for everyone to get together. Most of his men wouldn't even be awake yet.

Finding Cajun passed out on the couch, he kicked his boot. "Church in an hour," he lit a cigarette and let it hang from his bottom lip. "Help me call in the troops."

Grunting, the Sergeant at Arms sat up. *"Mais la!"* he let out. "It's dawn."

"It's ten. Come on." Dash kicked his foot again before he headed toward the back door.

Cajun took out his phone and a pack of cigarettes. "Still fuckin' dawn."

Rounding up a bunch of bikers, who had partied all night, before noon was like herding blind, deaf, kittens. Between Cajun and Dash, they must have smoked an entire pack while they paced the patio behind the clubhouse calling, texting, and re-calling their club brothers. This was important shit. They had a big break in getting Whiskey back and delivering Tut and Jackal to Nástrond.

For the first time in his life, Clark arrived at church on time. Hell, he was there before everyone. Sitting at the head of the table, looking like a greaser out of the book *The Outsiders*, the president stared at the emblem etched into the wooden table. His gaze had that fire Dash was getting far too accustomed to seeing.

Taking a seat beside him, Dash snapped his fingers. "Hey. Guys are rolling in. Should be able to start on time."

Clark blinked and focused on him. "Where are they?"

"A warehouse in Medina." His leg bobbed up and down with nervous energy.

Medina was about forty-five minutes from their clubhouse. Forty-five fucking minutes. They had some balls setting up so close.

"Is Whiskey good?" the leader asked, cracking his knuckles.

"Seems so." Dash shrugged.

Whiskey hadn't spent much time talking about his condition. He focused on what the Roughneck Riders had let him know and what he could share. True loyalty. They owed it to him to get him out of there as soon as possible.

Their brothers slowly filed into the room, and the conversation between Clark and Dash halted. Most of the men appeared as though they'd just rolled out of bed—bleary-eyed, unkempt hair, and wrinkled clothes. By the time everyone had taken a seat, the room they used for church smelled like a damn locker room. An hour wasn't enough time for them to drag their asses out of bed *and* take a shower if they wanted to be on time. At least they'd made it.

The gavel came down to start the meeting.

Lifting his chin, Clark inhaled audibly and looked every bit the part of the confident president of a criminal biker gang. "One of our Montana brothers brought us some information. He's solid. I'd trust him with my life, your lives, and Monty's life."

Bringing his hand to his beard, Dash twisted a small section below his lip. He nodded in agreement as he considered Whiskey, the only black one percenter he'd ever met. The guy had more fucking stones than anyone.

The president rolled the gavel in his hand, allowing the weight of what he said to hit the men. "So, we know it ain't bullshit and we're going to need to put it to a vote what action we're going to take."

He glanced toward Dash and deferred to him to share what Whiskey had told them about Tut and Jackal. Their location, their numbers, and the tricky part–their businesses.

Knowing most of these men had history with Tut and Jackal, most positive, it wouldn't be the easiest of pills to swallow. He did his best to keep his face stern, void of the emotion broiling beneath him.

"It seems they're focused on cheap and easy cash." Dash shifted in his seat as his gaze landed on Odin's profile on the table. "Heroine, pills, meth, and pussy."

His brothers grunted around the table.

"Who's their source?" Cajun said.

Taking a heavy inhale, Dash met the somber hard expressions one by one around the room. His brothers didn't play. They wanted blood. "The Flores family."

It hit the room like Thor's hammer. Eyebrows raised and several men sat back. A few scrubbed their bearded faces.

Mooky cursed. "They're fucking bad news. Bowie had a deal with them a while back."

"Crazy bastards," Cajun added. "All 'bout the dolla', no loyalty."

Meeting Clark's gaze, Dash nodded. No loyalty could be explored. Crazy made for bad business. Sitting back, Clark tapped his index finger against the gavel and the weight of the club seemed particularly heavy on his shoulders that morning. He ran his hand down his freshly shaven chin. "We take out their operation, we're gonna have trouble with the Flores family."

"You offer them a better deal," Mooky said. "And they will drop Tut and Jackal like a bad habit. They did it to Bowie."

"Bowie did it on purpose," Cajun drawled. "He wanted out so he purposely made the deal bad so Flores would drop out."

"Dropped out with no fallout?" Clark asked skeptically.

The room collectively shifted in discomfort.

"It was bad," Mooky offered. "They let us know they

weren't pleased. We lost a few brothers, but eventually they moved on. Got bored, I guess."

Dash nodded. *Bored, or moved on to Tut and Jackal.* There was no way of knowing when this bullshit with them and the Flores family started. This was one of the many things he agreed with the national president about—drug lords.

Drug cartels were not known for their stability. This was why Monty wanted no part of drugs. Not to mention the heat that came down when a club started peddling them. They didn't need that much attention. *No one* needed that much attention from law enforcement, local or federal.

"We owe them a visit," Clark said. "But we can't do shit until we sort out the Flores situation."

Grumbled agreements circled the table.

"Mooky, Cajun, go." Clark pointed toward the men. "See what you can see. Send a message."

Both men nodded in the affirmative. Send a message was code for do damage, but don't kill. The two selected were known for their ability to do just that or further if given the order.

Groaning, Clark took in the room. "Well, we're here. Any new business?"

"We got four new prospects and then there is the matter of Chuckie. Could vote in the prospect," Dash shrugged. "He's been busting ass."

"Doesn't ask questions, just does what he's told," Mooky leaned back in his chair.

"Solid shot," Cajun shrugged.

Clark twirled the gavel in his hand. "Any objections to Chuckie getting his colors?"

Mumbles, shrugs, and nods of agreement went around the table. Chuckie had what it took. He'd make a good brother.

Unanimous decision, Chuckie would be patched in later that day. Clark slammed the gavel down to close out church.

"Laissez les bon temps rouler!" Cajun smacked the table with his open palm. "It's been too long since I sent a good message."

CHAPTER 8

Gingersnap

$\mathcal{E}$verything annoyed her. The errant string of her scrub top, having to reheat her leftovers a second time because the middle was still cold, and even the tight bun in her hair was not behaving. All of it kept her on edge. Liz knew she was irrational. She just couldn't stop feeling irritated.

How dare he just go back home? How dare he not discuss it with her? No, he just sent her on her way like they weren't working toward a relationship. They spent far too much time together to *not* be working toward something serious.

She slammed the silverware drawer as she thought about it. "Asshole."

She should have known when she saw the vest. The stupid cut. Bikers were assholes when it came to women. The show depicted them that way. That *wasn't* exaggerated.

Lifting her chin, she huffed. She should be happy that he'd taken it so cavalierly. It meant she wouldn't be cheated on. If he went home, then he wouldn't be around for her to get attached and there wouldn't be any opportunities for him to get attached either.

That's another thing she saw both in the show and learned from the little research she allowed herself about bikers. They were not known for their fidelity, but that didn't mean they didn't get attached. They seemed to want their women to be faithful to them, but they could do whatever they wanted. Fuck that. Liz was monogamous. When she invested, she was all in.

But with whom? Dash or PRK? They were more than just two nicknames for the same person—hell they were more than just two different personalities living in the same person. It felt like they were two different people.

PRK, a play partner. PRK was on the kinky side and Dash was the other side he showed. Dash was the guy who took her to dinner. PRK was the guy who wouldn't let her wear panties around him. She could deal with PRK. Finding a competent dominant in Ohio seemed like finding a fucking rainbow unicorn.

So, it begged the question. Dash or PRK?

There was no good reason to cut her nose off to spite her face. She could keep him at a distance. She could cut off this emotional bond at the knees and keep it strictly kink. She'd be damned if she dealt with Dash again. Nope. When her phone chimed, showing she had a text message, her stomach fluttered. Immediately cursing herself for the hope that it might be him, she angrily tapped the phone to see that it wasn't.

Ane.

The fact she was disappointed ticked her off that much more. She hadn't even known him very long.

ANE

Hey chickadee. What are you doing after work?

Normally, she'd be with Da—PRK. *PRK*, she reminded herself. But tonight? Nope. Tonight she would go out with her friends. Spending most nights together would stop. She'd keep it to play dates at the public play space. No more private sessions. Too much opportunity to slip into feelings. She didn't need feelings for a guy who would leave.

LIZ

Nothing. You wanna get drunk?

ANE

Does the Tin Man have a coke can cock?

She snorted. Ane and her eloquent way of letting Liz know she was always up for booze and a good time.

LIZ

Cool. I think you'll like this place. The Broken Spoke.

Okay, sure. There was a huge likelihood they'd run into PRK, but maybe that was the point. She wanted to show him she didn't need him to have a good time. She'd lived in Ohio for quite some time before he ever showed up. She knew how to have fun before he came into her life. She could do it again.

Maybe she'd hit on one of the other bikers. That was taboo, right? According to what she saw in the show, it wasn't a good thing, but so what? He was leaving. Okay, she wouldn't be a complete twat-waffle, she'd make sure they weren't in his club. She'd avoid anyone wearing a cut that matched his. But the way she saw it, any other guy who rode a motorcycle was fair game.

ANE

Don't know it, but I'll be at your place
at 9pm.

LIZ

Bring Puppers.

She'd need all the support she could get.

ANE

Like we could go anywhere without him.

LIZ

Nowhere fun.

ANE

LOL keep that to yourself. He'll think he's the
life of the party or something.

She adored her friends. They were always there when she
needed them. Granted, they didn't know she needed them—
or maybe they did. Great friends became like family, and intu-
ition in families was a thing. Perhaps her friends had devel-
oped a spidey sense or something. It didn't matter. Come hell
or high water, they were having a good time tonight.

After locking her door, she headed down to her car. Six
patients were on her schedule for the night. Hopefully, it
would go quick. With drive times, and how long it took to
tend to them, she should be able to get done by eight. That'd
give her ample opportunity to get ready for her night out.
Everyone knew nothing good happened before ten.

As she checked her eyebrows in the vanity mirror, the
vrrr vrrr of her vibrating phone caught her attention.
Expecting another message from Ane, she checked the
screen with a smile on her face. It fell immediately at the
name of the caller. Rolling her eyes, she swiped to ignore it.

Nope. Not today. She tossed her phone in the center console and grabbed her bag.

Liz wasn't in the mood to deal with that right now. Firing off a text saying she was on her way to work would be enough. Her mother was against talking on the phone or texting while driving.

The rattle of her phone vibrating in the cup holder confused her. Her mother normally didn't respond when Liz told her she was in the car. That was enough for her. So, at the red light, she checked the phone.

DASH

You going to be at your place tonight?

Dash. That was a Dash message. PRK's messages were far more flirty and sexy.

LIZ

Going out with Ane.

DASH

Club business has me wrapped up. Don't think I'll be around.

LIZ

K

She fired back and put the phone down. Of course. How stupid she'd been thinking this was more than it was. He was temporary. This was him slowly pulling away. First, he blew her off for "club business" and now "club business" conveniently cropped up again. Sure.

Her phone rattled again, and she ignored it.

Nope. She shook her head at the phone as though it would give her more resolve.

That was all he needed to know. *He wanted to keep her on a*

*stupid need to know basis, well two could play at that game. How
did he like it?*

He was leaving. He'd need to get used to their separation.
He made that decision without discussing it with her, well
now she made a decision without discussing it with him.

"How do you like that?" she said to the phone, knowing
full well he wouldn't hear her.

SHE LEFT her phone in the car when she went into her
appointment. Taking it in with her would be far too much
temptation to respond or check what he said. She told
herself it was far more professional to leave it behind. A
distracted nurse was an ineffective nurse. These were
people's lives, she couldn't take risks. Nope. Her personal life
was a mess. She didn't need to make her professional one a
dumpster fire too.

Afterward, there were two texts from PRK and one voicemail. Well fuck. She couldn't leave those notifications
unchecked. They'd taunt her like an inner ear itch—impossible to scratch. What if something had happened? Her mind
cycled through a series of scenarios, all of which involved
him laying his bike down in a ditch somewhere and being
taken to a hospital and her being his last contact. So, the
hospital workers were reaching out to her.

Blowing a strand of unruly fire from her unkempt messy
bun away from her face, she shook her head in frustration.
She couldn't in good conscience ignore him—not with those
possibilities out there—even if they were unlikely.

"Hey, it's me. I know you're working. Text me if you don't
want to call."

Calm, cool, collected. There wasn't a sense of urgency in
his tone, but there was a bit of authority in the deep timbre

of his voice. No messages from hospitals—just texts asking when she planned on going out and where she would be going.

Her inner submissive wanted to comply—wanted to answer him. She wanted to please him. She enjoyed pleasing him. Hell, it was fun to please him. But not right now. Nope. This was a lesson he needed to learn.

With an assertive nod of her head, she let her phone clunk back into the cup holder. She needed to keep reminding herself of the goal. She had to remember the point of all this. He did this. This hadn't been her call. If he had just talked about it, maybe she wouldn't have to play this game. He didn't get to ditch her without talking.

Communication, it was imperative for good play and it was imperative for relationships. Wasn't that one of his huge talking points when they were messaging back and forth before they met? Hadn't he been the one to tell her there was no point in even getting involved if they didn't communicate? He didn't follow his own advice.

She glanced down at that phone. "Well you suck at it!"

Yeah. You tell him when he can't hear you.

She shook her head at herself. While at the stop light, she snatched her phone and tapped at her apps. She needed to hear some female empowerment songs. She needed some stuff to keep her focused. Meredith Brooks *Bitch*. Christina Aguilera *Fighter*. Halestorm *You Call Me A Bitch Like It's A Bad Thing*.

Liz frowned after she added it to her playlist. Halestorm. "No."

She shook her head and pushed the memories of their play sessions when he played the band. He didn't get to take Lzzy Hale from her. The phone went back into the cup holder as the light changed and her badass bitch playlist started.

By the end of her shift, she wasn't sure if she was angry or disappointed by the fact that Dash hadn't left her any more messages or texts. Between each patient, when she settled back into her car, she checked the phone. Each time, her heart sank a bit deeper. Nothing. Rolling her eyes at her own ridiculousness, she cursed herself for playing games. She just couldn't stop herself from doing it.

She needed the night out. She needed to take her mind off him. She needed the distraction from their situation. Okay, maybe not too much of a distraction. Maybe validation? Ugh, she didn't know. She just didn't want to feel this way—disposable and inconsequential.

"BITCH," Ane sang as she entered Liz's apartment. "You ready?"

After applying a deep shade of lipstick, Liz puckered at her image in the mirror. She was ready, all right. Clad in a tight jean skirt that showed off her legs and low heels she could walk in—yeah, it would definitely garner some attention. If that didn't work, the thin, cut-off Halestorm tank top she wore without a bra would definitely earn her some looks.

Yes. Halestorm. Was it a fuck you to Dash and PRK? Yes. She'd take the band back. Not that anyone would see, but she wore purple panties. Out of defiance, she would go to the bar that his club ran and wear panties. *Take that, PRK.*

Call it juvenile or petty, she couldn't decide. She didn't want to think about it. She'd done far too much thinking all day. Too late anyhow. She'd committed to it at this point. Her friends were there. It wasn't like she could change her plans.

Yes she could. No. She would do this. This was the plan and she would stick to it.

When she exited the bathroom, tousling her loosely curled hair, she grabbed her small wristlet purse. "Ready?"

Pupper lifted his brows, jaw dropping as he looked her up and down. Ane's mouth hung open for a moment before she grinned.

"If I had known we were trolling for ass, I would have worn my good jeans." Pup turned, peering over his own shoulder to look at his own butt.

"From the website, it didn't look like a place we would be," Ane replied sounding bewildered.

"What?" Liz asked, feigning innocence, still fluffing her hair. "I felt like getting dressed up."

"You mean slutted up," Pup said. "I'm gay, and even I know you're looking for dick."

She frowned. "No."

Not *a* dick. Attention. She wanted attention.

"Okay, well then, I need to change." Ane sauntered past Liz.

"Me too!" Pup followed behind.

Liz did a double take. "Wait. What are *you* going to change into?"

She understood Ane. They were close enough in size, but Pup?

"I'll find something," he called from down the hall.

CHAPTER 9

Dash

"You look *particularly* broody," Blue said as she sidled up to Dash at the bar in the clubhouse.

His phone laid on the bar next to his craft beer. It was some fancy local brew boasting notes of peanut butter and chocolate. It wasn't good, though he'd had worse.

"Got a lot on my mind." Like the fact Liz hadn't messaged him back or returned his voicemail. He wasn't a needy guy, but he didn't like not hearing from her. She always texted him back.

The prospect he'd stationed outside her apartment had told him she'd gotten home. So, he knew she hadn't gotten into an accident or worse. He'd also been informed who'd arrived. When the pictures came through, it confirmed what she'd told him—not that he'd ever assumed she'd lie. Dash swiped a hand over his face and curled his fingers around his beard. He didn't like her lack of response to him.

She's with her friends. Give her space to be with her friends. It wasn't like he could answer when he was involved with club business. Which should be his focus. He needed to get his head on straight.

Whiskey was still behind enemy lines. That's what he should focus on. Hopefully, Mooky and Cajun would at least get eyes on him to confirm he was still good. His brothers left two hours ago. They should hear from them soon. Messages weren't long drawn out things, but quick to the point, and back home.

"Want to talk about it?" Blue intruded into his thoughts.

Turning toward her, he dropped his hand from his beard and rested his elbow on the bar. Def Leppard played over the speakers while his brothers mingled with their guests—hang arounds and club whores. They laughed, played pool, and fondled one another. This was all good for business. Life returned to normal in Ohio now that the mourning period neared the end.

"Not especially." He took a sip of the beer and cringed. Damn aftertaste was nasty. He set it down and pushed it away.

Blue chewed on her bottom lip.

He put his back against the cool wood of the bar and wrapped an arm around her shoulders, pulling the woman against him. "What's on your mind?" He could use the distraction.

With her head resting on his shoulder, she sighed. "Mooky."

He should have put money on it. "Catching feelings?"

Sheepishly, she looked at him through her false lashes before reluctantly nodding.

Ahh, hell. The problem with tapping club ass on the regular pressed against him. He'd yet to meet one that didn't want on the back of a bike. It may not be *his* bike, like with Blue, but it was someone's. A few didn't discriminate and would take any brother who would have her. They tended to target the older guys, the fatter ones, and the less attractive ones. Others had tunnel vision. Blue fell into the tunnel vision category.

Dash mussed her hair and let her go. "Well, that's a bitch."

She groaned and looked out to the crowd of people enjoying the club's hospitality. "I mean, he has to have them too, right?"

Dash quirked a brow. This wasn't going to go well for him, or her for that matter. Letting a woman down wasn't high on his list of enjoyable activities. However, bros before hoes was definitely a thing with the club.

"Like, no one else approaches me anymore," she pointed out when Dash didn't verbally answer. "I could walk around here naked, fall to my knees with an open mouth, and not one cock would come my way."

The laugh that escaped him was unavoidable. Her rather accurate description conjured an amusing image.

"I wouldn't be opposed to testing that theory."

Her glare assured him that Blue's preference was for one biker. The scenario she'd painted wasn't something she'd do. Bummer. While Liz was the only one he wanted to play with and fuck, it didn't mean he couldn't enjoy some good scenery every now and then. Blue was damn fine scenery—plump and full in all the right places. She had curves for fucking years.

There was only one problem, Mooky hadn't claimed her officially. Everyone knew she was his favorite girl, which meant no one else would disrespect him and mess with her. So, the lazy ass didn't *have* to claim her.

"Do you know if…" She twisted the bottom of her crop top nervously. "Do you know if he likes…do you know if he's into me?" she asked with big doe eyes.

He hated those innocent eyes. Vulnerability wasn't a good

look for a club whore. Nothing softened a cock faster than a bitch who looked like a wounded puppy.

There was one place that look belonged. When his play partners gave it to him, like Liz, it got his dick hard.

The sluts, whose responsibility was to show the club brothers a good time, had no business giving that look while around the bikers. Annoyance flared within him, perhaps irrationally.

The women who came to the clubhouse knew what was up. The expectations were clear. There were no questions as to their purpose and why the brothers kept them around. Not every pussy that walked through the door snagged herself a biker. Some just rode the cocks that were offered. That was it, no matter how hard they tried for more. They wouldn't get it. If they pushed for more, they'd find themselves out on their ass.

He liked Blue, which made her catching feelings that much sadder. If Mooky didn't want her and she persisted, she'd lose her access.

Dash took a deep breath and turned back to the bar, flagging down the new prospect behind it. He held up two fingers. "Tequila, two."

Blue wasn't asking if Mooky liked her. A blind man in Toledo could see he liked her. When the shots came, Dash pushed one toward Blue. Faced with her hesitation, he nodded and lifted his own. Reluctantly, she took the small glass. Peer pressure at its finest. Together, they threw back the shots.

Her ample, most likely unrestrained breasts quivered with a shudder.

"Are you going to make me say it?" He wouldn't, but he could pretend. With the rhetorical question asked, he met her eyes. Most in her situation would settle for access and cling to hope of something rather than know otherwise for sure.

Her shoulders slumped. Turning her focus away, she scanned the room.

Using his thumb and forefinger, he twirled the empty shot glass. The moments passed while he allowed her to process his words. He suspected she knew how he'd answer, but took a shot.

He expected the dejected look in her eyes when she shifted her gaze back to him. "No," she admitted. "I know the deal."

Dash nodded. "How's your portfolio looking?"

While it appeared as a change in topic, he'd bring it back.

Nodding, she tucked hair behind her ear. "Good, actually. I'm getting so much better and learning a lot."

"So, it's not all bad," he reminded her. "You're getting something. He's getting something. The club's getting something. Everyone's happy." Her reason for wanting Mooky had been her desire to be a tattoo artist. The Enforcer had lived up to his end of the deal and hooked her up with the club's shop.

Movement caught his eye. He shifted his focus past Blue toward the red-eyed bull coming his way. Clark looked like he was about to rip the head off the next person who spoke to him. It'd be in everyone's best interest if Dash headed him off at the pass.

With a pat to Blue's shoulder, he grinned. "Chin up. It'll work out."

Granted, how things worked out would be up for interpretation, but that wasn't his decision. He'd let them figure it out. Either Blue would let sleeping dogs lie or she'd push. In the end, it wasn't his problem. He liked her, but if she broke the rules, there wasn't anything he could do. They existed for a reason.

He made a bee-line for the pissed off president.

"Office, now," Clark rumbled.

Without further words, the two made their way to the back office, which had once been Bowie's. In the short time between his hospitalization and his death, Clark had redone it. Gone was the hospital bed, oxygen tank, and bottles of pills. They'd been replaced with a new desk, new décor, but the same filing cabinets.

Once the door closed, Clark let out a feral roar and fisted the hair on either side of his head. "Gone. They're fucking gone."

"Who?" Dash didn't immediately connect. "Wait, Whiskey *just* called."

"They left in a fucking hurry." Clark rounded his desk and took a seat in the high-backed chair. "Left a bunch of furniture and booze behind."

Dash furrowed his brow. Running his palm over his head against the grain of the little bit of stubble which had grown in since his last shaving it. "Whiskey?"

Staring off, Clark balled his fist. When his eye twitched, he slammed a fisted hand on the table with another animalistic cry. "Wasn't there. They found a body. Think it's a prospect. Young kid, couldn't have been more than eighteen."

"Fuck." Shit must have hit the fan after the call. "But no Whiskey?"

Clark shook his head. "Nothing."

Dash dropped into the chair opposite the desk. Disbelief radiated in him. They'd had them. How the hell two yokels like Tut and Jackal kept getting the jump on them really chapped his ass. Frustration taunted his addiction. What he wouldn't give to smoke right now. Out of respect for Bowie, he'd not light up in what used to be his office. No matter how much he could use it.

The knock at the door penetrated the silence of the two of them stewing over their royally fucked up situation.

"Come in!" Clark hollered.

Dash turned to see Boxer, a member in the doorway. "Just wanted to let VP know his redhead bitch is at the Spoke."

The involuntary growl rumbled within him at the word 'bitch' used in relation to Liz. Boxer glanced with a puzzled expression.

In the club world, bitch wasn't exactly derogatory when referring to a woman. It was, however, not a good idea to use it when referring to a guy's Ol' Lady.

That was the thing. He hadn't made her his Ol' Lady, which made her just his bitch. He couldn't fault his brother for it and took a deep breath to calm himself.

"So," Clark said in exasperation. "That's not a reason to come busting in on a closed door meeting."

Shifting uncomfortably, Boxer pulled out his phone. "I think he might disagree."

He turned so the pair could see the screen and pictures of Liz and her friends. From a distance, chatting with some pansy ass Sunday Riders had Dash's blood boiling. *What the fuck was she doing? And why the hell hadn't the damn prospect told him about it?*

"Go take care of it." Clark waved.

CHAPTER 10

Gingersnap

"You ever been on the back of a bike?" Tom, the tall blond guy in the cut, asked as he leaned to press his shoulder against Liz's. She smiled at him, but it felt wrong.

His vest was far too stiff, and not nearly as soft and well-worn as Dash's. She'd also noted, despite the plethora of patches he sported, he lacked the 1% patch she'd seen on the Odin's Fury cuts. There seemed to be more men wearing the diamond patch as the night dragged on. She felt their eyes on her, but she did her best to appear unphased.

Perhaps that's why she leaned into him. If they were watching, she might as well give them a good show. She was somewhat of an exhibitionist, after all. "Nope. I've always wanted to, though."

He wasn't bad looking. He had a chin dimple. Liz wondered if Dash had a chin dimple. She couldn't tell with his beard. *What would he look like if he shaved it? He could be one of those guys with a really small chin and it could totally ruin his face. No. He definitely could never shave his beard.*

Okay, she needed to focus. She sat there with Tim—er Tom. She needed to focus on Tom and Tom didn't have a beard. He looked rather clean cut for a biker. Sure, he had the vest, but what he wore underneath, a tucked in button down shirt and jeans, didn't exactly scream badass. Dash was the epitome of badass, but he was leaving. Which meant she needed to stop comparing the two and stop thinking about Dash. So, Tom it was, if she wanted to get on the back of a bike.

"Nothing like it in the world," he said before he took a sip of his light beer.

Light beer. Such a pussy. "I've heard. You gonna take me for a ride?"

"No." The familiar dominant baritone startled her yet stroked her soul.

Jerking her head, Liz gaped, seeing Dash standing over their table with his arms crossed. The death glare aimed at poor Tom would have most shaking in their boots. Hell, she was intimidated, and it wasn't even pointed at her.

"Whoa, buddy." Tom held up a hand, leaning back from his canoodled position. "Not your bike." He grinned. "Mine."

She cringed internally at that word.

When the biker beside her resumed his position and wrapped his arms around Liz, her gaze never left Dash's. Her bald badass' narrowed gray eyes stayed on her as well. His left one twitched. This was about to get ugly and it was her fault.

"You going to get on his bike?" Dash asked in an eerily calm tone.

With her stomach in knots, and the guy she'd been flirting with nuzzling into her neck, she wasn't sure she wanted to answer that question. She didn't *want* to be on the back of Tom's bike. She wanted to be on Dash's but that wasn't a fucking option. He planned on going home to Montana sooner rather than later, leaving her with this desire for a badass biker.

"What business is it of yours?" Tom interrupted from his seated position.

Ignoring him, Dash merely raised his brow, waiting for Liz to answer.

She shifted in her seat, freeing herself from Tom's embrace. When she tore her gaze away from the dominant who knew all her buttons, she licked her bottom lip. Ane and Pup, where were they? They'd gone to get shots at the bar to give her private flirt time with Tom, but that felt like hours ago. One of them would've known what to say. Pup would know how to break the tension. He'd crack a joke or something. She panned the room for reinforcements.

Tom took her hand and brought her focus back to the situation in front of her. "Listen, I don't know what your deal is, but this is between me and the lady."

Without warning, Dash's hand went to the back of Tom's head and slammed his face onto the table. The innocent man's face bounced off it with a thump. Over the music and the conversation of the bar patrons, she heard a crunch. His nose, it had to be. She winced and covered her mouth. Reflexively, Liz recoiled away from the man she'd put in the unfortunate situation.

"Ahh. Fuck!" Tom crumpled to the floor. "Asshole." He held his hands close to his face as the crimson drops of blood flowed from between his fingers.

The rage in Dash's eyes, the wildness, it should have scared her. When he pointed at her, she held her breath.

"You and me are talking. Now."

With no room for argument, Liz stood and followed him to a stark back room. A small table with several chairs around it sat in the center of the space. The walls were lined with boxes labeled with what they contained, napkins, straws, and other such bar things. The door closed and he grabbed her wrist, whirling her around to face him.

"What the fuck?" he demanded.

"What?" She finally found her voice. She knew what, but she wasn't ready to admit she'd played a game. He had no business being mad anyway.

"You know what the fuck what." He gestured to the door. "What the hell was that? You came to my club's bar, and flirted with a fucking weekend rider?" he said through gritted teeth.

"You're leaving," she blurted.

He pulled back and the rage disappeared from his eyes. The fire was gone, replaced with a squint. Confusion was written on his face.

When he said nothing, the need to fill the silence between them overwhelmed her. "You got a call this morning. You're going back to Montana. What's the point?" She folded her arms over her chest in defiance.

Narrowing his eyes further at her, he put his hands on his hips. His continued silence made the music of the bar that much louder in her head, despite it being muffled by the closed door. With a snort, he cocked his head to the side. "I'm not going anywhere."

"I heard the call." His half of it, anyway. "You said how long."

He sucked in and licked his bottom lip on a deep inhale. "You overheard half of a conversation about club business. Instead of talking to me about it, you jumped to conclusions and you do this?" He pointed to the door. "Why?"

Unable to meet his gaze, she lowered her own, and held herself a bit tighter. It was a childish response. She knew that. Being put on the spot about it had her squirming internally. She didn't want to admit she'd been petty and wanted to hurt him.

"Liz," he growled in that dominant voice that always got her attention. "Look at me."

Slowly, she brought her gaze back to meet his, and fuck her. She could see the feral-ness in him. He wore his serious dominant expression and her body heated. It only got hotter when he closed the distance between them and took hold of her arms. Several inches taller than her, when he was this close, it made her crane her neck to keep eye contact.

"You're mine."

She'd never heard his voice dip as low or rumbly as it had with that possessive statement.

Her nipples tightened and she squeezed her thighs, yet she'd lost her voice and didn't know how to respond.

"Am I clear?"

She nodded, but the memory of Richard telling her the same exact thing danced in her head. It felt familiar—dirty, but at the same time, she wanted to hear it. She needed to hear it. She longed to belong to—confusion clouded good judgement. This was how she wound up in the situation with Richard.

"I said, am I clear?" he repeated.

"Yes, sir." Her voice shook as she slipped into submissive mode and the words fell from her lips involuntarily. She couldn't help it.

He did that to her, his presence, his voice, and the way he looked at her. All of it triggered that deep need to be under his thumb, to do what he wanted, to please him. There was something about him that took up all the space in the room —in her mind – in her consciousness. It intoxicated her.

"You will not do this again," he said and brought his forehead to hers. "You want to dress fucking sexy and come to the Spoke, you tell me. I'll bring you. You want to flirt with a biker, you text me, you call me. You're fucking mine."

His.

He kept saying she was his, and holy shit she wanted that. She thought she wanted that with Richard too. He promised that too. Then he used her. He used her to get what he wanted. What did Dash want?

"Yours," she whispered.

"You displeased me," he told her, pulling her head back. "You'll be punished. I won't tolerate childish behavior."

She gaped at him. If he used pain for pleasure, her mind raced with the ideas of what he would use for punishment. Nothing she could think of was appealing in the least bit.

Was that what Richard had done? Had the whole mess with Richard been punishment? There was nothing more unappealing than having her name dragged through the mud, possibly going to jail—punishment. Richard punished her by using her to commit fraud. How would Dash punish her?

"You have a problem, you will speak to me about it. This only works if we communicate." He released her arms and walked to the table.

Turning, putting her back to the door, she watched as her heart thundered in her ears, racing in her chest. Her breathing picked up and suddenly the room felt even smaller than it was.

"Bend over the table," he instructed.

Finally, she snapped. "Yellow!" Shaking, her eyes welled with tears. She couldn't do it. She couldn't live through something like that again. She couldn't have another man ruin her life again. "Yellow!" she repeated, because she couldn't bring herself to actually say the word to end it all. She wasn't strong enough to do that.

Dash stepped away from her, his hands up, palms toward her, peering at her.

Cowering under his scrutinizing gaze, she turned away and squeezed her eyes shut. "Please," she whimpered. "I can't."

"Liz," he said in a softer tone. This wasn't a command. His inflection was laced with affection, but he stood at a distance. "What's going on?"

She bit her lips together and sniffled. "I-I-I don't know." She took quick short gasps for breaths. Raising her hand, she covered her chest. On some level she knew it to be impossible, but she still felt like she needed to keep her heart from pounding through it.

Fluttering her eyes open, the world came into focus. She felt like the ground tilted. Dizzy, she knew she had to sit so she wouldn't hurt herself if she fell over. Sliding down the wall, she curled herself into a ball and hugged her knees to her chest.

He came closer toward her and crouched beside her. "If you don't tell me, we can't work through it. It's more than just you mishearing a phone call."

Mishearing? "You're not going back to Montana?" she asked.

"Do you think I'd leave without talking to you about it?"

Richard did all sorts of things without telling her. "I don't know."

He nodded. "I would not do that. I may treat you like a toy at times. I may enjoy playing with you." He cocked his head to the side. "But I respect you. I will never leave without telling you." He took a deep, audible inhale and ran his fingers through his beard. "There are many things I won't be able to tell you. I'll never leave you guessing though. If it involves my club, I'll tell you it's club business. You'll have to trust me. Can you do that?"

Could she? That was the question. "I—" She wanted to. Everything inside her screamed to trust him—her heart—her core—but her head hollered just as loudly that she'd trusted Richard and look what happened. "I want to."

He hummed and nodded. Sitting back on his heels, he appeared contemplative.

Silence hung heavy between them. The need to break it— to fill it with words—made her tongue itch. She just didn't have any.

"There are three pillars to every power exchange relationship," he said, and held up his hand. "Communication." His index finger popped up. "Consent." He arched a brow as his middle finger joined the other digit. "Last, we need trust." He held up three fingers. "Without those three things, we cannot move forward."

Closing her eyes again, she rested her head on her knees. "I know," she murmured.

"You yellowed," Dash said. "You didn't red. Do you understand the stop light system?"

"Yes." She nodded against her knees. "Green means go, all clear. Yellow means slow down, I need a break. Red means stop, I can't do this anymore."

"You yellowed."

"Yes."

"You didn't red."

She didn't say anything.

"Why didn't you red?"

Her breath hitched. "I don't...I didn't...I..." She lifted her head and met his stare after her false starts. This wasn't something she could say without looking him in the eye. He deserved that. "I'm scared," she said so softly it felt like the words came from someone else. "I'm scared because I've never wanted to belong to anyone the way I want to be yours. Even with my ex, I thought I wanted to, but never like

I want to with you. It's absolutely terrifying, but amazingly addicting at the same time. I'm terrified."

He nodded and extended his hand palm up toward her. "It is scary."

Her gaze flicked from his face to his hand and back again.

"Thank you for communicating your need to submit to me, your want to, and your desire to do such."

She took a deep breath and nodded in agreement. "I do want that."

"Do you consent to a power exchange dynamic with me, one that will include punishment if you do not continue to communicate with me effectively and utilize childish games instead."

Frowning she nodded again. "I will do my best to talk to you. So, yes."

"Do you trust me?" he asked.

Her heart skipped a beat so hard it lodged in her throat. *Trust. Could she trust him?* She trusted Richard. Studying him, crouched there, listening to her, and watching her, holding out his hand, waiting for her to make the choice. She knew in her bones he wasn't Richard.

"Yes. I trust you."

He grinned and she swore she saw some relief in his eyes. "Take my hand. We still have the matter of your punishment."

She nodded, and slid her hand into his. The callouses on his grazed her softer skin and sent a shiver through her body as he helped her to her feet. After giving her a gentle squeeze, he kissed her temple, and released her hand.

"Bend over the table," he repeated his previous instruction as he walked toward it himself.

While her steps were slow, she obeyed him. Once at the table, she put her hands, palms down, on it, and bent at the waist. In doing so, the skirt she wore rode up, barely covering her panty-clad ass. Panties. She'd worn panties—purple ones.

Resting her cheek on the cool table, she closed her eyes. His hand skimmed the hem of her skirt, which sat in the crease of her legs where her ass met her thighs. It took some tugging, but he got the skirt up over her butt, bunching it at her waist.

"Covering my work?" he tsked. "Though, I'm not sure what to make of your color choice."

She squeaked when he yanked the panties down to her knees, baring her ass to the cool air of the room. The dark purple bruising and welts he'd left behind from the previous night were clearly visible. When he brought his hands down to massage the sore flesh, she groaned.

"What is my rule about panties?" he asked.

"I can't wear them in your presence," she said on a sharp inhale.

"You're aware this rule includes purple panties?"

"Yes, sir."

"Yet, you defied me." His hand collided with her ass, hitting her just below the curve.

The sting sent her up on her toes and she whimpered as the sensation went straight to her clit.

"I was considering collaring you." His hand cracked down on the other cheek.

She yelped as her eyes welled with tears. Collaring her. Collaring her was a big fucking deal. She wanted it. She wanted to be his. She wanted that commitment. The ache to be collared by him pulsed in her chest.

"So obedient." He massaged her ass some more, but it didn't feel good. He paid particular attention to the areas he'd marked, and it had her lifting one foot then the other to escape the pain. "You had been so obedient. Now this."

SMACK.

"Ahhh!" she cried, and the tears fell. He'd hit her harder and hurt her more during play sessions. Yet she cried now. These weren't tears of pain—a deeper emotional release came with those tears.

SMACK.

Each sob he ripped out of her as his hand made contact with her took the burden of what Richard had left her with away—doubt, insecurity, fear—gone and she wept.

She grunted and pressed her forehead into the table while the tears dripped down her cheeks.

"You have been my perfect little toy. Then you do this." He dug his fingers into her ass and she squirmed against the table. "Do you want to stop playing?"

"No!" she practically screamed.

"Do you want to stop seeing me?" He squeezed.

"No!" She trembled against the table, pinned now between him and it, as the pain throbbed from her ass.

"What do you want, Liz?"

SMACK. SMACK.

"Ahhh!" She sobbed.

"What do you want?" he repeated.

SMACK. SMACK.

"You!" she gasped. "You! To be yours."

"Say it again." His hand cracked and the sound of it filled her ears as her ass burned under his attention.

"To be yours."

She had no defenses right now. He'd broken them down, broken *her* down. She cried hard into the table, ugly tears that ran her makeup down her face. She had never wanted to be anyone's as badly as she wanted to be Dash's in that moment.

Expecting another strike, she jolted at the feel of his hands on her hips. When he tugged, she stood and found he'd sat down and directed her to his lap. She sat. Her sore ass, sensitive to the material of his jeans, had her wriggling, but it only made it worse.

One of his arms looped around her back, and the other directed her head to nestle into his shoulder. "I don't play games. I don't expect you to either. I'll tell you when I go back to Montana. We'll work it out. I won't just disappear on you. You have my word," he said before kissing her forehead.

She nuzzled into him, kissing his neck and trying to catch her breath. The feeling of safety in his arms washed over her. The tears slowed and the sobbing had stopped. She still felt exposed and vulnerable in his embrace, but it didn't scare her. She trusted that he'd care for her in that state.

"You're coming home with me tonight." He stroked her hair. "We'll get your car in the morning."

"Ane," she whispered. "Pup."

"My brothers are taking care of them. Don't worry. You can text them before we leave if it'll make you feel better."

She nodded against him.

"I didn't bring my truck."

CHAPTER 11

Dash

Seeing Liz snuggled up to that jackass had tinged Dash's vision red. The guy was lucky he just got a broken nose. He wanted to do far worse, but didn't want to scare Liz in the process. Walking into that bar, the guy had sealed his fate as far as Dash was concerned. He'd never wanted to murder over a woman before. The shit she did to him.

He didn't play games, and he needed to cut that shit out with her. They were fucking adults, hell, he was thirty-two. He didn't have time for games. He'd only tell her once. When she'd told him why she'd done it, he had to be lenient.

He preached communication, which wasn't a lie. It was paramount for any kink relationship. Without it, there's too much potential for damage, not just play pain, or worse. However, when it came to his club, he couldn't be an open book. He'd tell her about his life, no problem. He'd tell her his feelings without a second thought. But club business. Nope. It wasn't her place. So, he took it easy on her.

Now that they'd gotten it out of the way, it was time to go home, and he'd be damned if he'd sleep without her tonight. She was his, Goddamnit. He walked through the Spoke, with her tucked at his side, holding his head that much higher. He'd never been a man to cower, but something about her made him feel taller—prouder.

So, it was high time he did something about that. The only woman a one percenter put on the back of his bike was his Ol' Lady—or the woman he intended to make his. Tonight, he'd let his brothers see her on his bike.

Practically vibrating at his side, she squeezed his hand the entire way out of the bar. He felt the eyes of his brothers on him. They knew what he was about to do. He'd hear about it, but he didn't care. Liz was worth it. She rewarded him with the most delightful squeal at the sight of his bike.

In the presence of his 2002 purple Road King, he let go of her hand. "Go ahead," he urged, gesturing toward his bike. "Meet the other lady in my life."

She chuckled and stepped toward it. Running her hand along the black leather of the seat, and over the swell of the gas tank, she giggled when she put her hands on the grips.

"I half expected you to have those giant handlebars, you know the ones you have to hold your arms up like this." She lifted her hands above her head. "To drive. I can't imagine that's all that comfortable. Doesn't the blood rush out of your arms?"

He chortled as he ran his hand through his beard before grabbing the half shell helmet and holding it out to her. "Ape hangers. I don't particularly care for them. I only have one, so until we get you one, you'll wear mine."

Hesitating for only a moment, she took it. As she popped it on her head, he walked around the bike and took hold of her hips to turn her. She looked small in the helmet. It didn't fit, but it was better than nothing.

"Riding on the back of a guy's bike is a big deal." He tightened the straps. "My brothers are watching. They'll know you're mine the moment you get on the back."

He'd seen the same doe-eyed look in Blue's eyes when she asked about Mooky. Seeing it now on Liz, on his woman, tugged at his chest. She was too good a woman for him, but he was too bad a man to let her go.

"I'm serious." He ran his hands down her arms. "Respect is king in my world. You absolutely cannot get on the back of anyone else's bike."

"I won't," she responded quickly and lifted up on her toes. At five foot ten, Dash wasn't the tallest guy in the world, but his woman, she couldn't be more than five foot six. .

Taking hold, he pulled her against him and crushed his mouth over hers. He slid his arms around and dug his fingers into her ass. She groaned into his mouth, and his cock stiffened. She'd be sore for a while but it looked so beautiful on her.

Dash nipped at her bottom lip and taunted her tongue with his own. The kiss was possessive and hungry. He needed her. The way she looked in that outfit, her hair, the makeup still running down her cheeks. And her ass, oh fucking God, her ass. If he hadn't felt so possessive of her, he'd throw her down on the ground and fuck her right there.

He didn't, because that would mean his brothers would see her. She wasn't a club whore. She was his and that meant his brothers didn't get any of her. All his.

Breaking the kiss, he cupped her face and forced her gaze to meet his. The look in her eye matched the need in him. The fire between them roared and he needed to get her to his bed sooner rather than later.

"I get on first." His raspy voice surprised him. "Kick your leg over and hold on."

She tried to nod, but he held her face still. He tilted her

chin down only to realize he couldn't kiss her forehead like he wanted. *Damn helmet.*

"Let's go."

One Month Later

THE SILVER INFINITY collar around her throat drew Dash's eye. He'd wanted to pay attention. She wore his collar on her neck. It marked her as his for the whole world. It called to him—distracted him. Vanilla people would see a thin steel band around her neck. It was discreet yet powerful. Perfect for his woman.

He'd given it to her two weeks ago. The same night he'd claimed her as his woman and the club voted her an Ol' Lady. He'd never expected to have one, but he couldn't have asked for a better woman. He didn't deserve her. His inability to pay attention to Ane's rope presentation at the Munch was proof of that.

"It's amazing that such a small woman can suspend such a huge guy," the woman across the table from them commented.

"It's all about leverage," Liz replied while she leaned back against Dash, giving him the opportunity to kiss the back of her head. Closing his eyes, he took a deep inhale of the coconut shampoo she used.

When he opened them again, he watched as Ane twisted, looped, and pulled the ropes she had coiled around Pup. The young puppy boy was on his side. His head lolled slightly. One of his arms was behind his back and his one leg was bent at the knee as he hung from the stand they'd brought in for the demonstration. Amused, Dash nuzzled into Liz's neck as he noted the half hooded eyes of the young gay man being suspended by the petite Asian woman.

"Next event, I'm suspending you," he whispered into her ear.

She shuddered, and she looked over her shoulder, before gifting him with a sly smile. He knew she liked rope. It wasn't something he had practiced all that much. He knew the basic ties, but suspension had been outside his skill set before he met her. He'd been practicing, though. He wanted to give her that experience. He wanted to give her all the experiences. Every kinky fantasy she had, he wanted to share with her.

AFTER THE DEMONSTRATION, with Pup wrapped in a warm blanket holding his bottle of water to come down from his rope high, they went to talk to Ane. With their fingers intertwined, they waited behind the small huddle. The group around Liz's friend fawned over her skill. It was well deserved with her talent.

Dash panned the room, watching others mingle and pack up to leave. As he scanned, he caught the back of a leather vest before the door closed. His blood went cold.

The skull with the miner's hat had a hammer and a large wrench crossed behind it. The image haunted his dreams. He'd seen that insignia before. He knew it far too well. They'd burned it once and now they'd do it again.

Tapping his woman on the shoulder, he leaned toward her. "Going out for a smoke," he whispered. He gave her a brief peck to her temple and moved away from her without waiting for a response.

"Now?" she asked. "But…"

He couldn't wait. Dick move, sure, but he had to.

"Dash!"

He winced. *Communication. Remember the pillars, fuckwad? He communicated. He could have a cigarette outside.* He trotted down the stairs after the man he'd seen and burst out the door while internally scolding and debating with himself. Once in the lot, he saw the tail lights of the Harley, and the back of the cut in the street light.

"Son of a fucking bitch," he hissed, taking his phone, his smokes, and a lighter from his pocket.

Dialing Clark's number, he pulled a cigarette from the pack, and placed it between his lips. With a flick of his wrist, he got the Zippo open and the flame lit. When he got the voicemail, he shook his head. Trying Cajun's number, he brought the red glow to the end of his smoke as he puffed it to life. Voicemail. He flicked the silver lighter closed before tucking it and the pack of cancer sticks away.

"Fuck!" he shouted as he swiped at his phone. Firing off texts, he paced in the lot, smoke coming from his cigarette in small puffs as though he were a steam engine.

DASH

> They're following me. RR's out tonight. Meet at the Spoke.

Pinching the butt between his fingers he rested his back against the wall. Life in Ohio had been too perfect the past few weeks. It's not that he'd forgotten about Whiskey, his brother was on his mind most of the time, but Liz had been an excellent distraction from the fact that when they went for him, he wasn't where they thought he'd be.

Unfortunately, it'd made Dash sloppy. Somehow, he'd not been aware he'd been followed. It begged several questions, who else had they followed? What else had they seen?

Tilting his head back, he banged it against the brick wall of the VFW where the munch met. He cursed his own stupidity and carelessness. He'd put his brothers at risk. He'd put Liz at risk by not being more alert. It wouldn't happen again.

He jerked his head at the squeak of the door opening. A cigarette dangled from his lip with smoke trailing up the sky. There was no doubt by the concerned expression on Liz's face that he looked as edgy as he felt.

"You okay?" she asked softly as she approached him.

"Yeah," he lied and reached for her. "Thought I saw someone I knew. Wanted to catch up." At least that part wasn't a lie. He'd gotten better at that, not outright lying to her, but also not telling the full truth. He was smoking after all.

Drawing her brows together, she glanced around the lot. "In Ohio?"

"Yeah." He forced a chuckle. "I know people."

With pursed lips, she gave him a skeptical look.

He pulled her toward him. Once against him, he wrapped his arms around her. He found solace in the fact that she was safe—for now. The idea that it might not be a guarantee taunted the edge of his consciousness and he mentally kicked it away. He didn't want to deal with that—think of it—least of all entertain it.

"Ane and Pup done?" he asked, changing the subject. After giving her a squeeze, he released her with one hand and took the butt from his lips while he blew smoke out of his nose. Dragon.

Dragons didn't take shit. Dragons didn't worry about shit. Dragons destroyed their enemies. Dragons got shit fucking done. Dash was a motherfucking dragon.

"Just about." She nuzzled into his chest.

He knew her well. If he surrounded her, pulled her into his space, she disarmed almost immediately. He should feel guilty for exploiting it.

"Let's all get drinks at the Spoke."

She grinned. "I'll go tell them."

He kissed the top of her head. Taking a deep whiff of her shampoo, he tried to let it soothe him as it had always done before. Replacing the cigarette to his lips, he nodded. "I'll be here."

CHAPTER 12

Gingersnap

*T*he night was warm for the season, but when on the back of a bike, going around sixty miles per hour, there was a bit of a chill. Liz cursed herself for not preparing for that. Dash had given her a hooded sweatshirt with his club's logo on it, but it did no good for her in a ball on her bedroom floor.

Hugging him tighter, her body pressed against his back. If it wasn't for the thick helmet he'd bought her, the patches would scratch her cheek. He'd bought her one that would be more appropriate on a motocross racer, but he'd insisted for her safety. It'd been the most adorable argument she'd ever had in a store. Recalling it, she squeezed her thighs against his.

As they slowed, he rested his hand on her thigh. Loosening her grip, she shifted back an inch to check out the status of the parking lot. The Broken Spoke had become their spot. The hole in the wall biker bar had grown on her and become her home away from home. His brothers knew her, called her Ginger, the nickname he'd had stitched on the hoodie he gave her.

His friends—brothers—welcomed her with open arms. They felt like her own. She felt like his world accepted her. She'd never blended into another person's space the way she had into Dash's.

Once the bike stopped, the engine cut, and he tapped her thigh, she dismounted. Over the last few weeks, she'd gotten better at it. She never realized just how awkward getting on and off a bike could be. It looked so easy on TV. The first few times she did it, she nearly ate concrete. Now though, she wasn't graceful, but she no longer lost her balance.

She pulled the helmet off and handed it to him. Pup's hatchback pulled into the lot. Grinning, she finger-combed her hair, trying to restyle her now squashed locks. There was nothing like having her friends mingling with her boyfriend's friends. While she may not let him hear her refer to him as her boyfriend, she definitely thought of him as such.

"Think we have time for a quickie before they get over here?" Dash asked as he wrapped her in a bear hug and took hold of her ass.

Squealing, she raised up onto her toes before he lifted her off the ground. Snaking her arms around his neck, she welcomed his kiss. For once, her ass wasn't bruised to high hell. Her tits, on the other hand…that was another story. The healing stripes from his cane burned ever so deliciously when her chest smooshed against his, she groaned into the kiss. The marks he left behind were the reminders of their intense scenes—of how deep into her submission he took her. The days of lingering aches allowed her to relive those activities while living her vanilla life.

It must have signaled him to go harder, because his fingers dug into her cheeks, closer to the crack of her ass.

Which made her squeaks louder, her squirming harder, and the pressure and fabric rubbing against her sensitive chest that much more intense. Her head swam with the overload of sensations. To make matters worse, his kiss grew hungrier, needier as his teeth grazed her bottom lip. She may have been chilly on the ride over, but now she was on fire.

That fucker knew exactly how to push every button she possessed. At this point she was convinced he installed new ones.

"Get a room!" Ane shouted as they approached.

"Seriously, it's been months now. We're over it," Pups grumbled.

Dash broke the kiss, but kept hold of Liz with one arm as he turned to face them. Blushing slightly, she tapped her lips, checking to see if they were swollen. Public displays of affection hadn't always been Liz's thing, but with him, she wanted the whole world to know they were together. She took every opportunity to be near him, to touch him, and he seemed to have the same possessive instinct when it came to her.

"Some of my brothers are in town from Montana," Dash said. He released his grip on her ass cheek to take her hand.

Ane arched her brow with interest. She and Pup had been very willing to hang out at the Broken Spoke lately. Eyeing her skeptically, Liz wondered if she had interest in a biker or perhaps Pup had. The idea of her friends hooking up with one of Dash's brothers thrilled her. In Liz's fantasies, they all became one big happy family, but not the multiple wives kind. No. She didn't want to share Dash that way.

With a quick pop across her ass making her yelp, she got out of her head.

"Let's get inside." Dash said as he took her hand once more and led the group into the bar.

At the door, Vinny, the prospect and current bouncer at the Spoke nodded while he patted down another guy. Liz had gotten used to this. When Dash was around, she and her friends got special treatment. They didn't have to show their ID's or get patted down for weapons. They went in. Even when she showed up to meet him there, Liz skipped the pat down. The club, new and prospective members, knew who she was. She tried to not let it go to her head.

Like the clubhouse most nights, the bar was filled with bikers, their women, and those who wanted to be bikers or wanted to be the women of bikers. The only difference being that every cut in the bar didn't have an Odin's Fury logo on the back. The bar, she'd learned, was considered neutral ground. Liz had noticed the only cuts in the Spoke that had the 1% patch were Odin's Fury. The more time she spent with the bikers the more nuances about their world she learned. She never imagined there were so many rules for men who had reputations for being rather chaotic.

Pulling her closer as they weaved through the crowd, Dash kissed her temple, before whispering in her ear. "The fights start in about an hour."

Not that one could whisper in a very busy bar, but he'd tried.

He'd told her about the fights a few days ago. The bar hosted bare knuckle boxing matches. Considering they weren't a casino, she was almost positive it was illegal with the amount of bets happening. Looking over her shoulder, she realized she hadn't told her friends about the fights. She extended her hand for Pup.

The younger man's eyes were scanning the room, so it took Pupper a moment to realize Liz's offering. Once he took hold, he reached for Ane, and their little train snaked through to the back of the bar.

A group of tables had reserved signs on them. Club members and their women always had a place to sit, even when the bar was standing room only. Apparently, fight night was a standing room only night.

As congested as the bar was, people still made room for them—Odin's Fury—and by association her and her friends. She wasn't sure if she was still riding high from the caning or the VIP treatment she got in the Spoke, but Liz felt like a queen herself.

The crowd buzzed with anticipation and Liz fed off it. Prospects took bets. Weekend riders talked shit about the upcoming matches. There was more on the line than just cash—bragging rights could be more valuable at times. Most of all, the men were drinking beers and throwing back shots. The bar was alive with business. The entire place pulsed with an energy which had her tempted for another bathroom tryst or backroom session. She made a mental note to suggest it later when they were settled in their seats.

By the time they reached their table, meeting up with some of his brothers, Liz practically vibrated with excitement. She'd never seen boxing live before, nor had she watched it on TV. On her own, it'd never interested her, but with money changing hands, people thrumming with excitement, and being in such close proximity—yeah, Liz definitely had an interest now.

"You know Clark, Cajun, Romeo, and Sparrow," Dash introduced. "That broody guy on the end is Mittens."

Clark gave his signature intense stare with a brief nod in greeting as his gaze drifted down toward Ane and Pup.

"Ah *cher*, always a pleasure," Cajun drawled with a wide, charming grin.

The woman in his lap wasn't introduced. Nor did she move as he gave a small salute to Liz and her friends. She seemed preoccupied with leaving a hickey on his neck.

"Come sit near me." Sparrow jumped up from her chair only to plop herself into Romeo's lap.

Romeo let out a groan of surprise before wrapping his woman in a tight hug. "Hey Ginger."

The man on the end, with his dark hair cropped close to his scalp, stared off into nothing. His square jaw clenched, visibly ticking as Liz assumed he ground his teeth. His fingers ran along the taped knuckles of his opposite hand while he paid them no mind.

"He's fighting tonight," Dash whispered, distracting her from accepting the seat beside Sparrow.

"Oh." She nodded. "Well, everyone." She turned and gestured to her friends. "This is Ane and Pup."

"Hi." Ane offered a wave.

"Hey." Pup stuffed his hands into the back pockets of his way-too-tight skinny jeans.

"Got your text," Clark grumbled. "Let's talk." He stood and nodded toward Dash, freeing his chair. "Have a seat." He gestured to Ane.

Liz did a double take hearing Clark, and offered her man a brief pout. She hadn't gotten the chance to make her suggestion.

Dash kissed Liz's temple, and she couldn't help but give him half a smile. His palm cupped her cheek, allowing for his fingers to graze the silver collar she wore. When he pulled back, his hand lingered. He stroked her collar a second longer and winked. "Be back in a minute. Don't let Mittens scare you."

Mittens...ahhh broody guy with the taped hands. She nodded.

The smile fell from his expression as he followed Clark into the back room. The same back room where he'd spanked Liz when he found her there hitting on other men. It seemed like a lifetime ago. Which meant they needed to revisit that room and make a new memory. It was due. Decision made—she didn't have to worry which place to choose, bathroom or backroom—backroom it would be.

Slipping into the chair next to Sparrow, Liz watched as Ane took Clark's recently vacated seat. Mittens stood with a grunt. "I gotta get ready." Liz glanced at Pup and patted the newly open chair. "All yours, kid."

"I'm gonna go get some beers. Who needs 'em?" he asked, pointing to everyone.

"We have a server. So sit your cute ass down. Ow!" Sparrow squealed, looking at Romeo. "Why did you pinch me?"

"Because the only ass you are supposed to notice is mine." He grinned while tapping her vest. "Property of Romeo."

She rolled her eyes. "I can look," she said, flipping wild wavy multi-tonal brown hair purposely in his face. "I just can't touch."

Ane and Liz couldn't help but snicker. Reluctantly, Pup took the seat beside Liz. The smile on his face seemed forced, which made her frown. She scanned the room, wondering just how accepting of him they'd be. Dash knew her friend's preference for other men, and had absolutely no issues with it. Regarding his club, her boyfriend hadn't said either way, but Liz wasn't so sure all bikers were that tolerant.

"You okay?" she asked, leaning into Pup so only he could hear her.

He jerked, as if surprised. "Huh? Oh, yeah. I'm in a bar full of leather-clad men, this is my fantasy."

He smiled, and it was much more genuine—but...

CHAPTER 13

Dash

Once in the back room with the door closed, Clark faced Dash. "Did you see who it was?"

The VP shook his head. "Don't know when he got there, only caught him leaving."

"Ginger see him?" his president asked.

Another shake of Dash's head. He ran his hand along the smoothness of his freshly shaved scalp. "I don't think anyone would have noticed he was out of place."

After he nodded, Clark scrubbed his hand down his face. "How are these fuckers out in the open and we can't get them?"

The defeat in his leader's voice crushed Dash. He wondered the same thing. They shouldn't keep getting the jump on them. Odin's Fury was the bigger club, the more experienced club. They shouldn't keep getting outsmarted.

A knock interrupted them. As the door opened, Cajun popped his head in. "We got company."

"Fuck," they hissed in unison before exiting the backroom.

"What now?" Clark sighed.

Stalking toward the table where he'd left his woman, Dash scanned the room, looking for anyone who didn't belong. Their bar was neutral ground. Colors could be worn with the understanding there'd be no trouble. The majority of the non-Odin's Fury cuts were riding clubs. They weren't the same. Rarely did another 1% enter their bar, and when they did, it was on the express invite.

When he spotted them, they stood out like sore thumbs. Their expressions were hard as their eyes locked on the table in the back where the brothers of Ohio sat. If the crowd didn't part for the out of place men, they shoved people out of the way without a second thought.

Jackal, the older of the two, zeroed in on Clark. Tut, the younger doofier of them, followed and met Dash's gaze. Two other men had their backs, and behind them, Whiskey. Relief washed over the VP. His brother was there and looked good.

But he couldn't let that show. He needed to keep the ruse now more than ever. This bold as fuck move would be their goddamn last. Blowing Whiskey's cover now would make everything he did for naught. No. He had to keep it up.

You're getting out soon, brother. Just hold a little bit longer.

Dash crossed his arms over his chest as he stood beside his woman. Oblivious to the threat walking toward them, she chatted with Sparrow and her friends. He didn't need to glance down the table, he knew that his brothers held the same death glare he did as the enemy approached.

With a sleazy smile, Jackal clapped his hands together once he reached the table. "How are you all doing?"

Shifting Sparrow, Romeo put her on the chair so he could stand. Cajun sent the woman who'd been in his lap away with a pat to her ass.

Clark rested his thumbs in his belt loops with his chin tilted upward. "Got a lot of balls coming here."

Liz and her friends exchanged confused looks. Sparrow knowingly tapped them and urged them away from the table, talking about shots. With a nod of permission, he tried to convey that she needed to go.

"Ah. Neutral ground," the former brother, the man with a price on his head, said nonchalantly.

His confidence had Dash's eye twitching.

"Got a guy to get in those fights." He reached into his pocket.

Stiffening, Dash rested his hand on his gun, ready to pull and fire if he had to. The bar was packed and it would draw far too much attention, but he wasn't about to stand there stupidly as the rat bastards mowed them down.

From his pocket, Jackal pulled a stack of hundreds.

Dash's finger twitched against the grip of his gun. He clenched his teeth. The only thing which could've pissed him off more would've been if the fucker had the nerve to pull a weapon. He had the gall to think they'd let anyone he sponsored fucking fight.

"Entry fee," he said with a wink. "And a little extra."

It took every bit of restraint he had within him not to pull his Glock. He was an excellent shot and as close as Jackal was, it'd be a clean hit. No one else, well maybe his fucking idiot son, would've been injured, but no. It'd bring too much goddamn heat.

They were in public. There were too many citizens around, too many wildcards. Fuck him sideways he had to play this straight. He had to be the prime fucking example of think before you act as the vice president of this mother fucking chapter.

Not one of them reached for the money. For the most part, it would appear as though they didn't even notice the offer to pay more than double the fee. The attempt to flaunt their success fell on deaf ears. The blatant disrespect to show up in their house, cocky as all fuck, was heard loud and clear.

"Denied," Clark said.

Lifting his brows, Jackal pulled the bills back. "Never known a club to turn down money."

"There are more important things than money," Dash snapped. The Roughneck Riders didn't know fuckall about that. They didn't know then and, obviously, didn't know it now. Well they'd learn. He'd make sure they learned.

With a hearty chuckle, Jackal nodded, stuffing the money back into the inside pocket of his cut. "Can't argue with you. Which is why you should all understand my actions."

"Fuck you," Cajun hissed.

As though in unison, the hackles of the men behind Jackal rose. They shifted on their feet, stiffening, and eying the officers of Odin's Fury through beady, hate-filled eyes.

"Now now." Jackal held out a hand. "That's no way to speak to your elders. Why don't we have a sit down?" He gestured to the back room. "Maybe we can come to a deal."

"No," Clark said.

Lifting his chin, Jackal shifted his jaw as he eyed the president. The smugness was gone from his face, replaced with annoyance. "We can mutually exist."

"No," Clark repeated.

Taking a deep, deliberate breath, Jackal's gaze scanned down the line of brothers, his former brothers as they stood in solidarity with their president. "You're making a huge mistake. I've got powerful friends that will make your lives miserable and will end your club at my say so."

Cracking his knuckles, Clark rocked his neck left and right until it crunched as well. "Odin's Fury fears no one. Especially you and your piddly ass club. Your *friends*?"

"Bring 'em." Cajun said.

"What'd you say?" Tut stepped forward.

Dash got close to him. Tut was about an inch or two taller, but far doughier. Dash worked out an hour or more a day. He sparred. There wasn't a doubt in his mind that he could take Tut out with little effort. Jackal took hold of Tut's arm.

"Neutral ground," the older man reminded his son.

"It's only neutral because *we* declared it neutral," Clark announced as his gaze panned to the other patrons.

The tension was thick between the two MCs and those around them gave them a wide berth while they watched intently.

"I'm declaring right now that no wannabe MCs are permitted in the Broken Spoke or any Odin's Fury owned business."

"Fuck you!" Jackal hissed as his stubby finger stopped just short of poking into Clark's chest. "My brother opened this bar. My club has a fuck ton more right to be here than you. Your club ain't shit."

"The Roughneck Riders are no more," Clark said plainly, purposely antagonizing Jackal.

"Riders Forever. Forever Riders!" Jackal shouted, his gaze going to Cajun as the men behind him repeated his cry. "Apparently, some of you forgot that."

"I ain't forgot nothing. My club, my brothers, my loyalty," Cajun offered. "My club patched over because it was best for the club and I don't regret it."

"Get the fuck out of *my* bar," Clark hissed.

Jackal curled his fists while his features vibrated in rage. If he'd come there believing he had the upper hand, he needed to have brought more than two other guys. The numbers weren't there. He started a war he couldn't win and knew it. It's why they hid and why they approached on neutral ground.

"Let's go." Jackal snapped his fingers, his men turning to leave. "This ain't over."

"It's only just begun," Clark said.

In a line, the men of Odin's Fury stood, defending their territory on principle. They didn't follow the Roughneck Riders out. Instead they watched them retreat, their tails between their legs. The fact it hadn't broken out into a fist fight was a miracle. Then again, no one wanted heat on them.

As the witnesses dispersed, Liz cautiously approached Dash. She looked over her shoulder as he reached for her.

"Who were they?"

Tucking her against his side and taking a deep inhale of her hair, the coconut notes soothed him slightly. She was safe —for now. Their boldness was rivaled only by their stupidity. That combination led to unpredictability.

He kissed the top of her head while trying to sort out exactly how to respond.

"People who won't let shit go," Sparrow said.

Glancing in her direction, Dash nodded in approval. Thank fuck for Sparrow—she had the words he didn't. Romeo held her protectively. His young club brother had no respect for Roughneck Riders. They'd done his woman wrong.

"People you don't need to worry about." Dash curled his finger under Liz's chin and tilted her face upward. "You won't see them here again."

"So, I thought I'd scored a number," Pup announced as he approached the group. "But this shit doesn't make any sense. Only thing I can make out is this superman logo."

"Give it to me," Clark yelled, his hand shooting toward the younger man.

Quirking a brow, Pup cautiously handed him the slip of paper. His gaze darted between the bikers and then to Liz.

After rubbing Liz's arm, Dash kissed her forehead again.

"I gotta see it." He stepped closer to Clark, reading the now unfolded note.

In code, Whiskey had written *Flores not happy. Bring a better deal, you'll cut RR off at the knees.*

CHAPTER 14

Gingersnap

*T*he night at the bar went from laughing and the mingling of friends to tense and foreboding. The agitated mood of the men lingered despite the company. The offending bikers may have left, but the vibe among their own group never returned. The men insisted on staying at the bar for the fights. Mittens was scheduled to fight after all. So, Liz did her best to cheer Dash up—to distract him.

While sitting in his lap, she kissed along his neck and up to his earlobe. He pulled away to sip his beer. She suggested the women, and Pupper, do a round of blowjob shots. They did them with no hands. He never stopped his hushed conversation with Clark. In her final attempt at flirtation, she figured she'd go for broke.

"So, I had this idea," she said once he'd stopped talking to his club brothers.

"Yeah?" Dash said as he peeled the label of his fancy craft beer.

"Mmhm." She nodded as she pressed her body against his

to bring her mouth closer to his ear. "I thought maybe we could go to the backroom and we could, maybe..." Her words trailed off as her hand slid over his thigh to rest on his dick.

He jerked, turning sharply at her. "What?"

His startled response nearly bumped her off his lap. It was enough to have her pull back while she bobbled slightly to keep her balance.

"Fuck, Liz, not tonight." He shook his head. "I just—I'm—I can't. Not here. Not tonight."

She saw the unspoken apology on his face. It didn't take away her disappointment. She took a sip of her drink to hide her frown. Nodding, she put her bottle down. "I need to go to the bathroom." She pushed off his lap.

"I'll go with you," Sparrow said, practically jumping out of Romeo's lap.

It hadn't been the company Liz had planned to take to the restroom with her, but who was she to complain. "Sure," she said as she made her way around the table.

In the bathroom, Liz tried to get information out of Sparrow about the men who'd ruined their evening. Sparrow didn't offer more than a shrug. "It's club business."

Club business. Dash had mentioned something about club business before. He'd said that it wasn't *her* business. She should have been more wary of it when he first mentioned it, but at the time, it made sense. Now, though, it seemed far heavier than she knew.

After the fight, which was far more brutal than she'd anticipated, Dash curtly told her he'd take her home. Part of her didn't want to go, part of her wanted to have fun. The other part knew there wasn't any fun to be had at the Spoke.

Even the ride to her apartment felt off. He didn't put his hand on her thigh. A little thing, sure, but she noticed. He always rested his hand with fingers splayed on her leg when they rode together. A sinking feeling settled into her gut as he walked her to her door. Especially because he didn't pull an overnight bag out of one of his saddlebags.

"Wait." She stopped.

He promised her they'd talk, and they needed to.

Standing at the base of the stairs leading to her apartment, Dash peered at her. "Did you forget your purse?"

"No." She hadn't brought a purse. "What's going on? What's wrong?"

She wrapped her arms around herself protectively.

Taking a deep breath, he averted his eyes, scanning the surroundings. He ran his hand over the top of his hairless head before he brought his focus back to her. "We can talk inside."

"No." She held up her hand. "Tell me now."

His lips tightened, making them almost disappear between his mustache and his beard. "Inside."

The tone caused the butterflies in her stomach to swoon. That tone normally called to her, turned her on, and made her want to obey whatever he'd said. She'd given up panties because of that tone, but this wasn't playtime.

"Tell me," she said defiantly. "I need to know what I'm involved in."

When she didn't move and only made more demands, his hand ran through his beard. A car door slammed. He turned, watching a woman on her phone head to another apartment.

From the inside pocket of his cut, he pulled out his cigarettes. Drawing her brows together, she watched him take one out, rest it on his lip, and spark it to life. Smoke plumed around him as he puffed before he clicked the lighter closed and put the items back inside.

The two of them stood there, staring at one another while a cavern grew between them. She didn't understand it and was only a few seconds away from begging him to say something. She'd begged him for plenty of things before, so she knew how to do it. Those other times were slightly different. For one, there were far fewer clothes. Biting her lip, she held off and waited. He'd have to speak. Eventually.

"You're not involved in anything," he said, passing her to ascend the stairs.

Doing a double take, Liz realized he intended to go to her apartment whether or not she went with him. She chased after him. "Bullshit. I'm involved because I'm with you."

At her door, he held the cigarette between two fingers while smoke came out of his nose. "I'm not a good man."

He seemed to study the red glowing end of his smoke. "You don't need the heat connected to me."

The odd juxtaposition of him at her door, leaning against the doorframe and her but a few feet from him only made the situation that much more awkward. "You've been nothing but fantastic to me," she said refuting his claim.

Heat? What the fuck did he mean by heat?

"Who were those men?" she asked.

He lifted his gaze to hers. "I know about your ex and the shit he put you through."

Gaping at him, she felt exposed in the worst way. There was far too much to unpack in those three sentences.

He ran a hand over the back of his bald head. "Everyone connected to us gets a background check. I know he tried to incriminate you in some identity theft shit and that he's locked away." He paused and twisted a small section of his beard below his bottom lip between his fingers as he laid out her most embarrassing secret.

Blinking, she wasn't sure how she was supposed to respond to all he'd said. She'd always envisioned being the one to tell him. She'd actually lost sleep over how she'd tell him. Having *him* tell *her* about her own past—there were no words for how it felt.

"You are too good a woman to get wrapped up in that shit." He looked away and she swore she heard him mumble. "Or in my shit."

She narrowed her eyes. *Oh no. He doesn't get to do that.*

"Wait a minute. My ex is in the past." She lifted her chin. "You had no right to—"

"For the club, I had to." He jerked his head back and while his words cut, his eyes held a softness—almost an apology.

She cleared her throat. "I want to leave my past in the past."

He nodded and once more turned away.

"You've been wonderful to me." Her mind swirled with things. She couldn't follow his logic or what was happening —was he—because of Richard or because of his club?

The way he looked at her when he turned back—she didn't like it. She couldn't read him. His expression was blank, but not hard. The lighting outside didn't help matters.

"Let's go inside," she suggested, pulling out her keys and reaching for the doorknob.

His hand covered her wrist. "No."

Alarms flashed in her head. The two of them stood there in silence while a frog croaked in the distance. Cars whooshed by. A moth fluttered to the street light. The two of them stood facing one another in some sort of standoff.

"I'm not good for you." He put his cigarette back in his mouth. "You deserve better."

Her heart seized. "I think I'm the one who decides what I deserve."

Shaking his head, he let her go and stepped away. "Not in this. It's my responsibility to look out for you. I have to take care of you. Staying involved with me will do nothing but ruin you."

He walked toward the stairs. She had to stop him. She had to make him stay. She couldn't let him go. This couldn't be the end. They weren't done yet. It didn't feel done. They were happy together. Happy couples didn't just stop being couples.

"Are you breaking up with me?" Her voice cracked with emotion. Out of pride, she wouldn't chase after him.

At the top of the stairs, she watched as a huge cloud of smoke floated about his head. His hand fisted, shook, then tapped the railing. "I have to. For you."

Without turning back, he walked down the stairs. With her mouth partially open, she stared where he had once been. She felt as though there was a gaping hole in her chest. Her stomach knotted and she was afraid to move for fear she would shatter. Tears welled in her eyes at the sudden loss.

Slowly, she reached up and ran her hand along the silver band around her neck. He didn't take it. He left the collar. He didn't ask for it. He didn't mention it. He just left without an explanation. He promised they'd communicate, yet…she felt like there was far too much that hadn't been said.

Swallowing the giant lump in her throat, the tears fell. Closing her eyes, she found the strength to put the key into the lock and turn the knob. Once inside her apartment, she closed the door, leaned against it, and slid down to the floor, sobbing.

Dash

MOUNTING HIS BIKE, Dash hung his head. The pressure in his chest made it hard to breathe. That was the last thing he ever wanted to do—end his relationship with Liz. Starting his bike he knew if he stayed any longer in that parking lot, he'd go back. He wouldn't be able to end it, but he had to. It'd be the only way to keep her safe.

He had to trick the loose cannons into thinking she was just a piece of club ass. If she wasn't around, she wouldn't be at risk, but they'd already seen her. Which meant he'd already put her at fucking risk.

Taking his phone from his pocket, he tapped the screen. Once again he called upon the most trusted prospect.

"You remember that address?" he said once the other man answered.

"Of that place?" the prospect asked vaguely.

Dash nodded as though he could be seen. "Yeah. Need you to go back. Keep her safe."

"You got it."

Dash ended the call. Twisting the throttle on the bike, he fought the urge to look back. It had to be done. He had to watch out for her—to protect her—even if that meant from himself.

CHAPTER 15

Dash

Three Weeks Later

*H*er property vest hung in his closet. Dash had planned to give it to her on a special night. There hadn't been one worthy enough for it. Now, it peeked out from the door that didn't close all the way, taunting him.

There wasn't a night where she didn't star in his dreams or a day when she didn't dance through his thoughts. Every redhead who walked by caused a double take. Since he purposely avoided places she'd go, he'd yet to see her.

To make it worse, he'd suggested Basketball Tits dye her hair. With his hand on the back of her head as she bobbed up and down on his cock, it didn't work. The color of the hair didn't trick his brain or his body. She was a poor replacement. She didn't swirl her tongue the right way. The slurping coming from her reminded him of porn—not his woman. The phoniness of it immediately turned him off.

The only thing she had in common with Liz was her persistence. His woman had texted him every day for the first week. It took everything he had not to respond. She tested his restraint, his resolve, his conviction. It was in her best goddamn interest. It was his fucking responsibility to keep her safe, goddamnit. He had to do it.

That's how he wound up with Basketball Tits slobbing his knob. In an attempt to distract himself, he'd chosen her. It'd be rude to text one woman while another had his dick in her mouth. Dash may be a lot of things, but he did his best not to be rude.

Liz may have stopped reaching out, but the club whore kept at it. Up and down, up and down, faster, slower, faster, more suction, less suction, with hands, without hands. Was that the back of her throat? Yep—cue the fake gagging. She was on a mission. Just like his submissive had been until he fucked it up.

No.

No. He didn't fuck up. He protected her. He did what he had to do. Jackal and Tut were two half-witted imbeciles with a death wish. They took risks without regard for their own safety. They didn't plan so it made it hard as fuck to predict their movements or figure out their next strike.

So he did the only thing he could do to keep Liz safe. He ended their relationship and put a club whore on her knees to try to get his woman off his mind.

The harder the slut worked, the more he compared the two. She couldn't hold a candle to Liz.

"I've been down here like an hour," Basketball Tits complained as she sat back on her heels and brushed her fake auburn hair out of her face.

"I'm pretty sure I'm five minutes from lockjaw." Everything about her was a sham.

"What the fuck, dude?" Exasperated, she lifted her brows in expectation.

Coming out of his Liz-obsessed thoughts, he glanced

down at his half chub. Nope. Would not happen. She wasn't doing it for him.

"I think I had too many." Bored with it, with her. He reached for his beer. Another thing he'd taken to since his last night with Liz. He'd started drinking light beer. Fucking piss. It'd never come close to his craft beers, but he needed to punish himself for what he'd done—or something. He might have to watch an episode of *Dr. Phil* or one of those TV shrinks to understand why he made the change from delicious to disgusting.

"Yeah, it's the beer." Rolling her eyes, she pushed up to her feet. She searched the room for her clothes.

He didn't blame her. As far as he knew, she wasn't blind. Staring at the vest in his closet, he tilted the beer bottle up and emptied the swill into his mouth. On the periphery, he noted Basketball Tits pulling her tank top back on.

He didn't even like fake tits and hadn't been the one to take her shirt off. She had done it. Apparently, she thought it would help the cause. If anything, it hindered it. His pants were still open, and his now flaccid dick rested against his thigh.

"You're no daisy," he quoted one of his favorite movies. "You're no daisy at all."

"Well, you're a prick," she snapped as she stood at his door. "I don't know what Blue sees in you," she said as she stomped out of the room.

Letting his head fall back, he pinched the bridge of his nose. Headaches had become a thing. He suspected sleepless nights were the cause. He needed to push Liz out of his mind. She was another thing that would not happen. He'd do better focusing on club business than his love life.

Tomorrow was the sit down with the Flores family. It'd taken far longer than he'd wanted to get it set up. They had to tap the older brothers, the lingering ones left over from the patch over, to work out the details. Precious few had much in the way of information. Perhaps that had been a testament to the type of president Bowie was, only those who needed to know, knew.

Eventually, Dash tucked himself back into his pants, stood, and zipped his jeans. No need to have it hanging out if it wasn't going to be used. He grabbed his phone. The disappointment that he didn't have a text or a missed call slapped him in the face, like it had every time he looked at it.

He tried to write it off as being tied to Whiskey, but truly it had nothing to do with his brother. Sure, there was a sliver of that. He was doing dangerous shit for his club, but Dash knew Whiskey could handle himself. Considering his brother was a veteran, the derelicts in charge of the Roughneck Riders didn't stand a chance.

Tapping the app for his kink networking website, Dash sat on the corner of his bed. Of course, he had a message from Sandy, an overeager submissive claiming to be 'an absolute pain slut.' Her words. Not his. There were a limited number of women who got off on pain, and even Liz wasn't one of them.

She got off on submission. There was a difference. Nuances. People just didn't get it. He doubted Sandy was one of those unicorns who truly enjoyed it. Especially because her experience didn't include a long-time play partner.

He'd indulged Sandy with messages back and forth. She served as another attempt at distraction. This time, he didn't suggest a change in hair color. He just needed someone— something to occupy his mind instead of the redhead he'd given his collar. Did she still wear it?

Stop it.

SANDY

Perhaps seeing what you're missing will convince you to come to the play party tonight. I've seen you there before. I'm up for a scene if you are.

Attached to the private message were pictures of her in a plaid skirt that didn't cover her flat ass. She could use a cheeseburger or two. The strip of fabric that ran between the ass cheeks hinted at red panties. She'd tied a white button-down shirt just below her breasts, exposing her taut belly. At least she wore a matching bra and panty set, because the red bra was on full display with the open shirt. It shoved her modest chest upward, giving her an unnatural cleavage.

With her hair up in pigtails and tiny little bows, and black rimmed glasses, she completed her schoolgirl look. Staring at it did nothing for him. The innocent schoolgirl look had never been his thing. He was in his thirties, for Christ's sake. He liked his women as adults, not cosplaying kids.

The more he looked over the pictures, the more his disappointment increased. He'd never realized he had a thing for redheads. It'd never popped up before. Also, her ass didn't call to him. Flat and unenticing, it didn't beg him to use it.

Though, as he sat there, shirtless, in his clubhouse bedroom while the men partied below, he thought of the sit down for the following day. The muscles in his neck tightened. Whiskey strolled through his mind. Dash's chest knotted. Basketball Tits' exasperation at not being able to get him off popped in his head. His fingers curled into tight fists. He needed some kind of release and failed blow jobs weren't cutting it.

The lack of attraction toward Sandy could be an advantage. If he wasn't into her, he'd be more likely to keep it a one-time scene. He wasn't in a place for anything long-standing. Were his situation different, he wouldn't need to consider her. He'd be with Liz.

Glancing upward, the vest drew his eye again. Fuck. He needed to do something to get her out of his mind. Pushing off his chair, he went for his play bag in the bottom of the closet.

With a tug of agitation, he yanked it out and tossed it on the bed. He unzipped it, and dumped out the contents. Shuffling through the items, he realized he hadn't touched it since he'd taken it out of his saddlebag. Everything in it was meant for Liz.

Internally, he winced, recalling that night. His jaw ticked, a sign of his mounting tension. The memory of the crack in her voice haunted him. He heard it in his dreams. It twisted in his gut like a knife. That wasn't the type of pain he ever intended to cause her. He'd planned a wonderful night of caning and paddling. Maybe, if it had gone differently, he'd have given her that fucking vest. The Roughneck Riders stole that from them.

They'd done plenty to earn the club's wrath. Stealing his woman from him earned his personal ire. While they hadn't, to his knowledge, physically laid a hand on her—the prospect still watched over her—sleeping when she worked, they were the reason. Their actions ripped her out of his arms and out of his bed. He couldn't let them get away with that.

At first, he didn't care. He was a selfish prick. He wanted her and she wanted him. Simple. As the threat of the Roughneck Riders grew, the more he questioned it. When they showed up not only at the Munch but the fucking Spoke, he knew he had to do it. He had to protect her the only way he knew how, removing her from the threat.

Floggers. Wooden paddle. A single cane. Nipple clamps. Cuffs. A riding crop. The generic things. He stuffed them in his bag. He kept his items that packed a true wallop—the ones he'd used with Liz—the ones she liked in the closet.

He needed a release and he had a woman willing to give it to him. He could sit there and mourn the loss of Liz forever, or he could get back up on the horse and move on. Club whores weren't doing it. He needed something more. He needed to let his dragon out and beat some fucking ass. Sandy's narrow flat butt would do for one night.

CHAPTER 16

Gingersnap

Standing in a pair of black panties and a matching bra, Liz shuffled the hangers in her closet. Nothing seemed to fit her mood tonight.

Well, that was a lie. Her flannel jammie pants and the tank top she'd been sporting earlier fit her just fine, but she wasn't sure that was the appropriate look for the play party.

The play party she hadn't a desire in the world to attend. It was the first one since Dash had ended things with her. She had no business going. Let alone, agreeing to do a rope scene with Ane's friend.

"What's taking so long?" Ane's voice got louder as she came down the hall. "We should have left a half an hour ago."

Groaning, Liz pulled out a sapphire blue dress she'd bought with Dash in mind. He'd liked the way blue made her eyes pop. Those were his words. Now she held the dress up, considering it for a night of play with someone she didn't even know.

"First of all," Ane began as she leaned in the doorway of

Liz's bedroom with a glass of wine in her hand. "That dress is fucking awesome and I'm stealing it." She gestured toward it. "Second, it doesn't matter what you wear there. It's street clothes outside. You're gonna be down to your skivvies in the scene. As close to naked as you can get works best with rope. You know that."

Liz sighed, fingering the tag still attached to the dress. "I know. I just want to..."

She shrugged as words failed her. Everything that came to her mind shouldn't be said.

I don't want to go. I want to sit on my couch and eat ice cream. I want to scream at him and demand he take me back.

Her thoughts raced with what she truly wanted. None of it had anything to do with the dress, or the play party, or Ane's friend.

"I just want to look nice." She offered a weak smile.

"Then you have a winner." She pointed to the dress. "Nacho is already there." she said as she scanned through her phone with her free hand.

Nacho Master. That was his name on the kink site. The fact that he had 'Master' in his name should have been a red flag. Liz had made it a personal rule never to associate herself with anyone who called themselves an honorific—sir, master, etc. Ane vouched for him, though. How bad could he be?

With a snap, she tore the tag from the dress. "Here goes nothing."

The dress meant for Dash would now be worn for someone who went by the scene name Nacho. She hoped his humor extended past the terrible pun.

Stepping into the dress, she changed her outlook. She'd spent far too much time mourning the relationship. She needed to do what he did– turn it off. He'd spent all of five minutes ending their time together. It was time to get back out there. Nacho probably wouldn't rock her world, but he was a start. Tugging the form fitting dress up her body, she took a deep breath. By plastering the fake smile on her face, she was intent on turning the night around and having fun.

"What do you think?"

Ane glanced up from her phone and swept her gaze over Liz. "Hot as fuck. Let's go."

THE HEAVY BASS of the house music boomed out onto the street from the third floor of the repurposed factory building. It helped mask the cries of those playing inside. Ane bopped her head to the beat as they approached. Ascending the uneven steps to the ribbon gymnasium, the effectiveness of the music dwindled. The cries of a woman enjoying, Liz assumed, impact play grew louder the closer they got.

Once they paid the cover and passed the privacy screen, the wide open play space became available to them. Her view of the goings on were blocked. He was tall, well over six foot, thin, and wore his deep chestnut colored hair in a long ponytail. His brown eyes sparkled with a wide smile as he opened his arms for Ane to walk into.

"Finally." He wrapped her in a hug and gave a hard squeeze.

Liz's friend returned the affection and offered the man a kiss to his cheek. "I know, it's been far too long. You know how it is, work and demonstrations, friends." She sighed. "Life, ya know?"

"You must be Gingersnap," he said in a heavy Spanish accent as he released one woman and offered his hand to the other.

Ane grinned. "That she is." Pride laced her words.

Liz took his hand, giving it a quick shake. "Nice to meet you, Nacho."

With a dip of his chin, he clicked his heels in an old timey gesture. "Charmed."

"Did you get a hard point?" Ane asked as she scanned the wide open space.

For the first time in over a year, Pup hadn't joined them. Apparently, he had a date. A date on the night of the play party meant he'd met a very hot guy. However, that meant Ane didn't have a rope bottom.

Pup and Ane weren't romantically involved with one another. They scened together at events because they weren't seeing anyone else seriously. Their complementary itches needed scratching and Ane was in high demand to show her skills, so they obliged one another.

"Yep," Nacho responded. "Over here. No one's used it tonight, but then again, the beauty of this place is that there are plenty of hard points to go around."

As a ribbon gymnasium, aside from being a nice wide open space, by nature it was meant for people dangling in the air. While normally, the acrobats used ribbon and tangled themselves, on nights that the play party had the space, it was a bit kinkier.

The trio made their way over to the spot Nacho had indicated. Ropes, uncoiled and ready for use, rested on the cold metal of a small folding chair. Seeing the braided jute, she swallowed a lump in her throat. Simultaneously, her hand reached for the collar she'd taken off weeks ago. Emptiness settled in her gut as her fingers grazed her bare neck.

"You okay?" Nacho asked, getting closer to her. Concern filled his warm eyes as he reached to rub her shoulders.

"Yeah." Liz forced a smile and waved a hand dismissively. "Getting in the headspace, you know? I haven't been suspended in a bit."

"Since she dumped an asshole," Ane retorted, though her gaze seemed fixated on something.

Liz attempted to follow her friend's line of sight, but Nacho blocked her. Taking a moment to focus on him, she realized he held something in his hand. Lowering her gaze to see it, she peered at the nylon webbed collar as though she'd never seen such a thing before.

In truth, with its plastic clipping mechanism, he offered a generic, every-day dog collar. Something she'd seen hundreds of times without thought. Now though, as he stood there holding it out to her, offering it, she couldn't do anything more than stare.

Her heart revolted. Her stomach flopped. Even her mind screamed at the offensive item offered to her. The subpar collar was nothing compared to the steel she had at home hidden in the box under her bed. It was a pathetic replacement. *Did he expect her to actually wear that thing?*

"It's a play collar," he explained. "Just to help for headspace. You don't have to wear it if you don't want to."

Moving on, she reminded herself. Quickly, she snatched it from his hand and slid it around her throat. With a click, it was in place and she looked up.

Done. Take that. Moving on.

"How do I look?" she asked with her hands on her hips as she preened. It felt awful. The stiff nylon scratched at her skin and it lacked the weight of the smooth metal collar Dash had given her. Bile rose in her throat.

Jerking her head toward Liz, Ane smiled, but it seemed forced. "Far too dressed for what's about to happen."

Tightlipped, she frowned as she was obviously missing something. Liz tried to follow where her friend had looked one last time, but Nacho stood in front of her again.

"Let me just straighten it," he offered, pausing a moment before his hands touched it. If she didn't know better, it felt purposeful—like the two of them were working together against her.

Okay, now that was just paranoid. She was there to scene with this guy, so she needed to scene with him. *There had to be another reason he just stood there. Think.*

Consent. Give him consent.

With a nod, she gave him permission. He was about to tie her up. She might as well get used to him touching her. The idea made her gut twist. She needed to get over that quick.

The urge to know who had captivated Ane nagged at Liz. Was it Pup? Had he brought his date there? That didn't make sense. He would have told them. They wouldn't have been able to get him to shut up if he'd found someone to play with that he could actually date.

Taking a deep breath, Nacho stepped back to stuff his hands in his back pockets. "So." He began as his eyes roved over Liz like she'd been a steak served to him. "You ready?"

No.

"As I'll ever be." Another fake smile.

She had to muscle through this. Ane had once told her the best way to get over someone was to get under someone else. While she felt zero attraction to the lanky man reaching for the jute, there were worse people to consider. Besides, it wasn't like they'd sleep together. It was just play. What was some rope between friends of friends? She peeled her dress over her head.

CHAPTER 17

Dash

Sandy was loud as fuck. Too loud. Over the top, definitely faking it loud. Blood curdling screams from open hand swats to her ass were on the verge of ridiculous. Her purred pleas for more and harder sounded like a script from a bad porno. Nothing about this did anything for Dash.

The twenty-something blonde he'd strapped to a St. Andrew's cross wiggled her pink ass while he reached for his suede floggers. The heavy bass of the music inspired his choice. Florentine flogging was best done to a beat. With the way his play partner had been screaming her head off, she'd drawn a crowd. Since he was service topping, he might as well put on a good show for the spectators.

That was the thing about play parties—when one had a skill, it attracted onlookers. Dash had once argued that there was a bit of a voyeur and exhibitionist in every person with kinks. Especially in those who attended public events. On the spectrum, he felt a bit more exhibitionist than he did voyeur. Then again, a magnificent scene was a magnificent scene, and he'd been drawn in more than once by another Dominant's skill and a submissive's devotion. A couple truly in tune with one another danced a truly elegant tango.

Rolling his wrists, he bobbed his head, finding the beat of the dance music. Swaying slightly, he did a bit of a dance as he swung the floggers far from Sandy. This accomplished two things, one, it allowed him to establish a rhythm that he'd use while flogging her, and two, it built anticipation for the submissive. Were he doing this in private, she'd have heard the swish of the falls through the air. The fact that it would appear as though he were a showman could be considered an added bonus to some. Dash personally didn't care. Especially, considering he wasn't exactly known for his dance moves.

His focus was on Sandy, her body, and her reactions. She was the purpose of the scene. He had to read her to know where to go, where not to go, and what to do next. Paying attention to anything else would make it unsafe. However, when he scened, he had to be, at minimum, aware of people around him. Idiots came in all shapes and sizes, which meant they also attended kink events. He'd nearly wrapped a flogger around a throat or two on his backswing because an oblivious kinkster walked into his area.

Sure, Dungeon Masters and Mistresses were about, but one couldn't always rely on them. If they got pulled away for a consent issue or were being questioned by someone new, they may not be as attentive to morons unaware of the length of a flogger. One step. Two steps. Scream. One flogger landed across her shoulder blade. Then the other. Sandy pulled at the bonds and wriggled. He had to adjust to make sure he kept hitting his target. Her cries grew louder as he continued. Her squirming increased, as did the redness of her skin. Faster, in some cases, could be construed as harder. He moved faster. She called out to all the deities she knew as her knees buckled. Thankfully, the cross held her.

Pausing, Dash stepped closer to her, pressing his body against the heat of her back. He'd had her remove her bra, but kept her thong on. The thing was barely panties, so it didn't get in the way of his mission to beat her. Also, he didn't want her to think he intended to fuck her. No interest there.

"Breathe," he whispered into her ear as he held the two handles of the floggers in one hand and reached around to massage her breast with the other. "Tell me your color."

The play space required the stoplight system. He made eye contact with a Dungeon Master, clad in a leather kilt and vest, who had moseyed over to either supervise or enjoy the scene. He couldn't be sure.

Whimpering, his play partner sucked on her bottom lip. Allowing her head to fall back, he noted how flushed she'd gotten. Taking a moment, he went to his bag and retrieved a bottle of water. Uncapping it, he brought it to her lips. "Take a drink."

This woman wasn't a pain slut. He hadn't broken out anything serious yet. Someone must have told her that was what men wanted. If he used the cane on her, he couldn't even use half of the force he'd used on Liz. He wouldn't even leave a mark on Sandy's body at this rate.

"I need a color, darling," he purred in her ear as he took the water away.

Gasping, she nodded. "Y-y-yellow." She didn't sound too sure.

Dash glanced at the Dungeon Master to see if he had heard her. Lifting his brows, as though asking without words, he got a nod. Dash did the same as he put the water on the chair and returned to the submissive he'd tasked himself with for the evening.

"Yellow means I slow down." He wasn't really sure she could take much more. She was young, and new, and he didn't want her to walk away with an unpleasant experience.

She nodded. Licking her bottom lip. "I can take more, Daddy."

Dash cringed. If there was one thing he couldn't stand, it was being called 'daddy' when playing. He wasn't into age play. He didn't like children. It creeped him the fuck out. He knew there were some people who were into it, between consenting adults, not into kids. For him, nope. Hard limit.

In response, he cracked her ass with a good hard swat that made his hand sting. She screamed at the top of her lungs and tried to lift her foot, but the jostling of the cuffs holding her in place meant she couldn't move.

"Sir," he growled into her ear for correction.

When she didn't repeat it, another swat graced her other ass cheek. An ear piercing yelp came from Sandy.

"Sir," she hissed.

Taking a step back, he surveyed his toys. She'd ruined the mood with the floggers. He'd lost the pace and thus the interest, so he tossed them to the side. Rummaging around, he tried to decide how much longer he wanted to keep going. If he used the wooden paddle, he could build up and probably get her to go another twenty minutes. Lifting the acrylic cane in his hand, he patted it against his palm. If he used that, she'd last maybe a good ten, only if he went lightly.

While considering his options, he looked up to those watching, and considered getting input on what to do next. He was putting on a show after all.

His blood ran cold.

Upside down, her auburn strands grazed the hardwood

floor in nothing but black satin and jute. His woman dangled with her arms behind her back. Taking half a beat, he expected to see Ane as the rigger, but no. Some lanky ass fuck coiled ropes around the joint of her knee, no doubt in preparation to change her position with a good pull.

Grinding his teeth, the selection was made. Cane. His eye twitching, trying to quell his anger, he took deep breaths. Sandy's narrow, flat ass had lost most of the pink from earlier. Time to put some color there. However, he'd made a vow to himself never to strike a woman in anger. The rage he felt may not have anything to do with the woman he currently played with, but she'd still receive his wrath if he didn't calm the fuck down.

Rounding her, Dash faced Sandy. "Ready to be caned?"

He tried to shift his focus away from Liz playing with someone else and focus on the someone else *he* had in his care.

The fear in Sandy's eyes told him ending the scene quickly was the right choice.

"Yes," she said defiantly.

She wasn't ready for shit.

He tapped the cane against her ass with little force. It was enough to leave a little sting, but not nearly as hard as he wanted to go. The restraint he needed could only be accomplished by looking into her eyes.

Of course, she shut them. Gritting her teeth, she wiggled. He used about twenty percent of his force. Sandy was no pain slut. Attention whore, maybe. Bratty sub, definitely. Not for him—abso-fucking-lutely not.

Going to her left, he groped her now tender ass cheeks as he continued to cane, picking up the speed as he did so. No doubt, the sting increased due to the rapid falls of the narrow plastic against her flesh.

"Ahh!" she shrieked. "Ahh!" Louder that time.

He didn't ask what color. They weren't there yet.

Faster. Harder. Finally, he pulled back and popped her a good one and the red stripe went across one ass cheek to the other. The howl that came from her should have been music to his ears. For the first time since he met the woman, it might have been the only genuine sound which had come from her mouth. Had it been in a different tenor, and come from a sultry redhead, it would have been.

Panting wildly, tears streamed down Sandy's face. Bless her heart, she didn't safe word. She also wasn't enjoying it. Dash had no desire to continue to play with someone who didn't enjoy what he did. Sadist that he was, part of what made it fun for him was the person he did things to, enjoyed it as well—that whole consent thing.

He placed the cane down before he returned to her back. His full body covered hers while he massaged her butt. "Breathe deep."

Short raspy breaths would make her light headed if she continued. She nodded eagerly, and even tried to follow his directive.

Bending down, he gave a kiss to each ass cheek. She'd tried. She deserved some sort of reward. The hushed gasps from those watching usually made him chuckle when he opted to kiss the ass of the submissive who'd just taken a beating for him. Why wouldn't he reward a job well done or a valient effort? Some people thought dominants lived and died by their ego. Not him. He'd learned long ago the importance of being humble in the face of what a submissive allowed a dominant to do.

Hopefully, Sandy would learn from their session as well and would stop calling herself something she wasn't. Carefully, he uncuffed one ankle and then the other before rising again.

"We're done," he whispered, gently petting her.

"But." For some reason, she whimpered in protest.

She couldn't handle it. Why was she pushing herself?

"Shhh." He told her. "I'm going to release you. If you can't hold yourself up, I'll catch you."

CHAPTER 18

Dash

A fluffy blanket worked wonders for a submissive. The comfort brought her back to the present after her descent into sub space. The bottle of water returned hydration and gave the submissive something to concentrate on. Snuggles and check-ins conveyed safety. Dash followed all the steps he used for after-care despite the lack of need for such things.

Sandy hadn't slipped into sub space. Some might consider her endurance of the scene a feat warranting recognition. He suspected she was one of those, and it had to do with a misplaced understanding of what submission meant. Unfortunately, the far too common belief that a submissive just did what she was told without regard for her own needs was rampant. Submissives shouldn't endure a scene, they should enjoy it as much as the dominant. Dominance and submission only worked when the acts were mutually enjoyable by both parties.

As some of the other attendants approached to compliment them on the scene, he smiled to be polite. Rubbing her shoulder, he offered comfort as he listened to their admirers fawn. His gaze kept drifting toward his woman, though. His woman who let someone else tie her.

His.

Thankfully, the young woman in his lap spoke animatedly to her new fans, so he took that opportunity to tap her and nudge her up. She stood, mid-sentence, not stopping her chat and let Dash take the blanket off her.

"I'm going to clean up and put my stuff away," he said. He suspected she was too busy being adored to notice.

That was just fine for him. Wiping down the cross with the disinfectant cloths, he kept looking, but the circle that had once been around his scene now closed in on Liz and the asshole with the rope. They blocked his view, so he picked up his pace to get over there.

Once everything was put away, he slung his bag over his shoulder. He walked past Sandy. "I'm going to go check something out. Thanks for the scene."

If she said something to him, he didn't hear it.

A stern "excuse me" and maybe a little tap on a few shoulders was all it took for him to almost get to the front. That was, until someone blocked his path with a pissed off expression and her arms crossed.

"No," she declared as Dash peered down at her.

"I'm sorry?" he asked.

"You are *not* ruining this for her." Ane waved behind her without turning. "She needs this."

The twitch in his right eye returned as he looked past the dark-haired woman before him. With a tug, the man who scened with Liz tilted her body. Her nose was mere inches from the floor, but her bottom half would have been chest height for Dash. Her eyes were closed and a serene expression decorated her features.

"You left her." Ane's angry tone begged for his focus. She wouldn't get it. Not when his woman hung from the ceiling in another man's rope. "You don't get to take this little bit of peace away from her."

Drawing his brows together, he took a deep inhale. "There's more to it—"

"I don't care. No one cares," she interrupted. "*You* made a choice. Now live with it."

Narrowing his eyes, he tightened his jaw. Now she earned his attention. People didn't speak to him that way. Since the day he'd donned his cut, no one spoke down to him. No one reprimanded him with the malice Ane just did. Normally, he'd admire her moxy, but not when she stood between him and Liz.

"She's my woman," he growled.

"Not anymore," she countered. "You did that. Not her. Now, leave her alone or I will call a Dungeon Master."

Shifting his jaw left to right, he considered her words. No good would come from him having to tangle with a Dungeon Master. It'd ruin his reputation in the community. It'd get to Liz before he could. Bullshit like that traveled like wildfire. Unfortunately, it also became like a game of telephone. By the time Liz heard anything, it'd be so distorted from the truth, he'd never be able to speak to her again.

As much as he hated to, he held his free hand up, palm toward her. "I just want to make sure she's safe."

He did his best to look as though he surrendered. Not that he had any intention of doing so, but the impression that he had would go a lot further than if he hadn't.

Distrust wafted off Ane in waves as she glowered in his direction. She shouldn't trust him—he was a criminal, after all. He wore a one percent patch with pride. Granted, he hadn't worn his cut that night, but that was beside the point.

He'd stolen for his club, he'd maimed for his club, he'd killed for his club. In that respect, he wasn't a trustworthy man, and considering he'd ended his relationship with Liz, okay, yeah. He got it. He respected her resolve to protect her friend. Though, there wasn't a way he could show her how misguided her actions were. Of all the people in that room, Dash wasn't the one Ane needed to keep away from Liz. He'd done what he had to protect her.

He retreated a few paces to demonstrate that he'd heard her. He'd appear to back off, but it would be so as not to take that look off Liz's face. She did need it. He knew the hell he lived while apart from her. He knew she had feelings for him, so he knew it was no picnic for her either.

With his bag over his shoulder, he walked past the check-in desks to exit the play space. He needed a smoke to clear his head. Descending the uneven stairs, he debated if he should smoke one or five cigarettes as he tried to work through what needed to happen. When he opened the doors at the bottom of the stairs, he realized he made a wrong turn along his way. Standing in an alley rather than the front of the building hadn't been the plan.

For a moment, he thought of going to the front and smoking. He could head to his bike and just go back to the clubhouse. Then again, if he stayed there in the alley, the likelihood he'd run into Sandy diminished.

As he puffed his cigarette to life, he nodded to himself. The alley was the perfect place to plot. So, he leaned against the wall, focusing on Liz, and did his best to push the memory of the other man's hands on her out of his mind.

Gingersnap

Wrapped in the snuggly blanket, drinking the water, she stared at the floor. She'd curled herself up into a ball on the folding chair and shook off Nacho's attempt to rub her shoulders.

"You should probably get those ropes cleaned up before someone starts touching them," Liz suggested.

The rope scene had done wonders for her. The tension she'd felt at the beginning of the night left her the moment her body left the ground. The longer she hung, the more relaxed she'd become. To her, a suspension scene was equivalent to a deep tissue massage. It was, perhaps, the only thing she missed about Richard. He'd been an excellent rigger. In all the play she'd experienced with Dash, they'd never gotten a chance to explore suspension. It was on the list, the very long—seemingly ever growing list of things they wanted to do.

Things they'd never do.

The snuggles, whispers of encouragement, and the down time of after-care Nacho offered, weren't needed. She didn't want it, either—not from Nacho. While he'd gotten her into a state of bliss—it wasn't subspace. So her recovery wasn't the emotional kind. She needed the water, but everything else—nope. She never hit that emotional abyss where only Dash knew how to take her.

Ane approached. "Hey chickadee."

Liz smiled. "How was it?"

Chuckling, her friend crouched beside her and bumped her shoulder. "Shouldn't I be asking you that?"

Grinning, she leaned against her friend. "It was nice. Long time coming."

But her mind wandered to Dash. *What was he doing? Was*

he partying at the clubhouse or maybe he had beers with his brothers at the Spoke? She missed the Spoke.

"But, it could have…" She paused, not wanting to say more.

How could she say it could have been better? The guy she believed who would make it better had told her he didn't want her. Especially when Nacho had done an excellent job.

If she'd been anyone else who wasn't wrapped up in Dash, Nacho would be the holy grail of play partners. He knew what he was doing and had good friends to vouch for him. Yet, it wasn't there for Liz. She still longed for what she once had.

With a tight side hug, Ane rested her head against Liz's. "It'll get better."

Liz watched people flock around Nacho, complimenting him about the scene. Riggers got this often, and for good reason. Hours of practice, and years of work went into some of the things he could do. He deserved their praise and she was thankful it occupied him. It kept him from checking in on her. She needed the space.

"I'm going to get some air." Liz shrugged the blanket off and scanned the area for her stuff.

"Yeah?" Ane leaned back, giving her room. "Want me to come with?"

Shaking her head, Liz stood, found her shoes, and put them on. "I think I need some space to really bask in the afterglow of that."

She smiled weakly as she reached for her dress.

Going down the stairs in heels was a bad idea. The old building threatened to trip her with the uneven flights. Clinging to the railing, she made her way down to the landing without incident. Taking the triumph, she headed to the alley rather than the front because she really didn't want to deal with anyone. She needed to be alone.

The smell of smoke hit her as soon as she opened the door. Hopeful, she surveyed the darkened alley, lit by the lone flood light mounted high above her head. To her left, leaning against the brick wall, a cigarette pinched between his fingers, he stood.

CHAPTER 19

Dash

Had he conjured her? His brothers must have laced his cigarettes, because his woman stood there in a killer dress. The blue cloth accented every curve of her body to the point he couldn't believe this was real. As though frozen, afraid to move for fear the mirage would go away, Dash faced her.

She did the same, wearing the same shocked expression he did.

When she took two tentative steps into the alley, the door closed behind her with an unceremonious slam. The sound echoed. Something, somewhere knocked an empty can over and it rolled across the pavement. The silence between them made him hyper aware of every other sound. He swore he heard his heartbeat and hers because of it.

Without regard for the remaining cigarette, he tossed the butt to the side. He'd had two other ones before that, providing his system with more than enough nicotine.

Stalking toward her, he needed to touch her, to make sure

she was real. That was all. He'd just tap her. If she poofed into a puff of smoke, he'd give his brothers hell. Just a tap. That's all. Towering over her, he stopped with mere inches between them. Unable to stop himself, he took hold of her face.

She didn't disappear. Her warm skin was soft under his fingers. His pinkie slid down below her jaw.

She looked up at him with wide blue eyes. Gazing into them melted away any resolve or restraint he had.

He simultaneously bent his head down and tilted hers upward. The feel of her silken lips against his rocked him. Gentle at first, he cherished the feel of her. Soft and slow, he savored the taste of her pineapple lip balm. The more he sampled her, the more he needed.

Like an addict fiending for a hit, he lost it. She was his drug. He had to possess her. She was his.

She snaked her arms around his neck, returning the kiss after a few seconds. Taking his hands from her cheeks, he slid them down to her ass. Digging his fingers into her flesh, he vowed to worship it later as he backed her against the wall.

Breaking the kiss, he scanned her eyes. Fearing if he continued, he'd devour her, he searched for a reaction from her.

"I missed you," she whispered.

Her vulnerability in those words strangled his rapidly beating heart. Instead of responding, he crushed his mouth against hers, pushing her harder against the wall. *Missed her? Fuck, he'd been dying without her.* Hungrily, he growled into their kiss.

She moaned, scratching her nails across his back. Her chest heaved against his when he broke the kiss. Trailing nips down her jaw, her neck, and sucking on the hollow of her throat, he knew he'd lost all control. The fact that there was some sort of nylon collar on her neck only triggered his possessiveness further.

"Mine," he rumbled into her ear. "Fucking mine."

"Yours," she panted back.

The collar had to go. He hooked his finger behind it, between her throat and the nylon. His first thought was to tug it and rip it off her. However, in a brief moment of lucidity, it occurred to him that might not be a good idea, so he switched his focus.

He inched her skimpy dress up her thighs. He needed her. He needed to feel her. He'd lost his head, his sanity, and his mind for this woman. Once he had her ass exposed, he brought his mouth over hers again. One hand reached to undo his belt and his jeans.

Breaking the kiss, he pulled away, only enough to look into her eyes. "When I lift you, wrap your legs around me. I fucking need you right now."

She gulped and nodded. "Me too."

It wasn't romantic. It wasn't graceful. In porn, they made it look easy as hell. However, fucking his woman against the brick wall while he supported her weight was tricky.

Lost in the moment, the raw emotion of it, he pushed her panties aside, and sunk himself inside her warm, wet pussy. She gasped, and it spurred him on. Buried within her, he could only move his hips so much in that position. The ripples of her sex around his cock as he rocked inside her tested his will.

She grunted in his ear as he thrust harder, faster, and with reckless abandon. He couldn't think beyond burying himself deeper within her – somehow possessing her in this animalistic way was more than he could handle. Rationally, he hadn't been able to finish in weeks. Yanking himself out, he did his best to point himself down while holding her up. He should've apologized for staining her dress after he'd come.

He shouldn't have fucked her without a condom in an alley, either.

She took the pill. He wasn't concerned about that. He hadn't actually fucked anyone since her, so he knew he was clean. He trusted his woman that she'd be the same. If not, fuck, he'd deal with it.

But, what he could not do, is leave her unsatisfied. With her legs still wrapped around him, her back up against the wall holding her up, he'd use his hand. He bit back his own moan when his fingers grazed her hot slit. Freshly fucked, still swollen and aroused, she was sensitive and twitched against his body.

"It's just me," he whispered before he lowered his mouth to hers.

His fingers dipped between her folds, exploring her sex. He slid them along her lower lips moving upward. He matched her passion as she kissed him harder when his thumb grazed her clit.

Applying varying degrees of pressure against the nerve nubbin caused her to squirm. She panted and broke their kiss as she trembled against him. Her head fell against his shoulder when he plunged two fingers deep into her channel. "Dash," she whimpered into his ear.

"Mine," he said.

He thrust his fingers in deeper and wiggled them while applying pressure to her clit. Her walls pulsed around his digits. She sucked in a deep breath. Her body tightened against him. Holding her tight, he worked his fingers in the "come hither move" as she shook against him while her orgasm rolled through her.

Once it subsided, he slowed his movements before withdrawing his fingers. The moisture clung to them, and since he was a gentleman, he wiped it on his jeans before he cupped her ass with both hands to gently lower her back to the ground.

With the two of them now on flat feet in the alley, they panted in unison. Their gazes locked while they tried to catch their breath. He tugged down her dress and then cupped her face again.

"Come home with me," he said in a cross between a request and a statement.

"I've missed you so much," she said, pressing her forehead against his as she wrapped her arms around his shoulders.

Lifting her head, he kissed the top of it. "I can't live without you."

The collar caught his eye again, and he hooked a finger in it. It wasn't the collar he put on her.

"Play collar." Her throat bobbed as she swallowed.

Again, the twitch in his eye returned. "No more play collars."

It was his fault, and he'd atone for that. He pinched the plastic joiner, and the collar popped open. He slipped it off her and dropped it to the ground.

"We're going to your place to get your collar. Then I'm taking you home to make it right."

CHAPTER 20

Gingersnap

The lumpy mattress caused her body to ache that much more. Waking in the bedroom of the clubhouse always felt like she was in high school again, rousing from a sleep over in a friend's basement. It had to be the wood paneling on the walls and mismatched furniture. Nothing went together.

With a groan, Liz rolled over, expecting to collide with Dash. The empty side of the bed jarred her. Jolting upright, her gaze darted to the open bathroom door. They were comfortable with one another, but not *that* comfortable. He'd always closed the bathroom door before when he did his business.

"Dash?" she called, pulling the sheets up to her chest.

Nothing.

When she swung her legs over the side of the bed to look for her clothes, she spotted her phone and the sticky note on it. Pulling the square yellow paper, she read:

Club meeting early. Hopefully, quick. Breakfast when I'm done.

Taking a deep breath, she grinned. It wasn't that she thought he'd leave her there. He'd never done that before. Anything was possible in this place and while she may trust Dash, this clubhouse was a completely different ballgame.

Letting the blanket fall away, she got out of bed, walked around the foot of it, and checked the door. Locked. Perfect. She could shower in peace.

As she turned on the water, she thought about how they mixed their intense scenes with vanilla. While their intimate times did tend to be a little bit heavier on play time and power exchange, they still had sex without kink. They still spent time together like normal people. He'd taken her to a cute Italian place a couple of days after their first official date. They spent time with his club brothers playing poker.

Stepping into the shower, the warm water hit her, easing the sting of her achy muscles. It reminded her of just how content she'd become with Dash. Not that she enjoyed thinking of Richard, or likening Dash to him, but when compared, Dash seemed more competent on every level. He was a far better dominant and a far better boyfriend.

The more time she spent with Dash, the more flaws she saw in what she'd had with Richard and how much she'd settled. While not outright abusive, her ex-boyfriend was inattentive, singularly focused, and disinterested in anything outside of rope.

In retrospect, hindsight is 20/20, after all, it made sense. He wasn't actually interested in her. He was interested in the access she gave him. She was just a tool for him to gain access to victims and to commit his crimes. Dash legitimately had an interest in her. Dash felt like her Holy Grail of the kinky community.

Tilting her head up into the spray of the water, Liz couldn't wipe the smile off her face. He'd said he wasn't good enough for her, that he was a bad man. Dash couldn't be bad to her if he tried. The idea that he'd think himself bad puzzled her.

He'd served his country. He became a medic while serving—which meant that not only did he defend but he also cared for others. Those weren't things bad men did. Bad men exploited others for their own gain.

Shaking her head, she reached for his bar soap. When she put it to her nose, she got a whiff of the clean scent that often clung to his body in the time between showers and his first cigarette. The smell was always there, but often got masked by his habit.

Tiny bubbles trailed her skin as she lathered herself with his soap. As she cleaned her body, she couldn't help but be amused by the thought of how she covered herself with his scent. Were they in the animal world, others would know they were together.

When her fingers grazed the metal ring he'd re-affixed to her throat last night, she closed her eyes. *His.* She was his. She belonged to him, and it felt more right than anything ever had before.

BOOM.

The entire clubhouse shook while Liz was mid lather. The shampoo still in her hair dripped into her eyes as she forgot to turn off the water and almost slipped getting out of the shower. She clung to the curtain in an attempt to keep herself upright. Incoherent shouting from downstairs filtered up through the floor to her.

She snatched the towel from the rack and she wrapped it around herself as she crossed the bathroom floor. She skidded on the tile floor, this time she had nothing to save her. She went down and busted her ass. Pain rocketed up her spine.

Pop. Pop. Pop. Screaming. *Pop.*

"Dash!" She screamed and crawled to the door, abandoning the towel now. What did it matter? "Dash!"

Pop. Pop.

Frozen in place behind the bathroom door, her stomach dropped. Bile rose in her throat as her heart threatened to pound out of her chest. Gunshots. Those were gunshots. What the hell was going on?

Dash

HECTOR FLORES, the middle-aged man in charge of the family, sat with Clark and Dash as they hammered out the new deal. They'd provide the cartel with guns at a deeply discounted rate, ending their contract with the Roughneck Riders.

It'd gone well. They weren't quite at the point of taking a loss for the guns, but their profit margin was pretty tight. There wasn't a price for loyalty. Disloyalty needed to be punished. Jackal and Tut needed to suffer.

Step one - destroy their business contact. Step two—take them out. Step three—rejoice or some bullshit like that. Everything fell into place, finally. They'd get Whiskey out of there in the next few days for sure. Their brother would be back on his bike and going home. Dash could go home too.

BOOM.

"What the fuck?" Hector's thick Columbian accent came through in his surprise. Both of his body guards immediately pulled their guns.

Dash and Clark did the same.

"Stay here," the president of the MC ordered before he nodded to his VP.

The two barreled toward the office door, and down the

hall toward the shouts. Once they entered the primary room of the clubhouse, the shots rang out.

With his adrenaline pumping, Dash slipped into his soldier training and ducked behind a couch, dragging Basketball Tits with him. He held her in place while she flailed until she realized it was him. Sobbing, she wrapped her arms around his neck.

"Go out the back door, grab whoever you can, and get the fuck out of here," he ordered while peeling her hands off him. It took several tries before he freed himself. Once he got loose, he pushed her toward the rear of the clubhouse. She wasted precious time.

There wasn't time for hysterics. They were under attack. It was no place for women right now. Liz. His woman especially.

As another series of shots popped, he glanced up at the ceiling. He'd left her sleeping. She sure as fuck wasn't sleeping now. He needed to get up there.

Movement caught his attention out of the corner of his eye. He turned, pointed his gun, finger off the trigger, but right near it ready to shoot, when one of Hector's body guards crouch-walked toward him. They weren't supposed to leave the office.

"Go back to your boss," he growled.

It had nothing to do with them. Odin's Fury needed to defend their clubhouse. They had to take out whatever it was, whoever it was, who had the balls to go at them.

"He can shoot. He's fine," the man said holding his gun ready to defend the clubhouse with a wicked gleam in his eye.

Not having time to truly process Hector's man's glee, Dash popped up just enough to look around. Mooky held a bloody hand over his own bicep. Cajun screamed some

French shit Dash didn't understand into the face of someone lying on the ground.

Scanning, he noted the siege seemed to be over. The clubhouse had cleared. Five Finger Death Punch's *Jekyll and Hyde* played amid the mess that was their clubhouse. High tops and stools were upended. Standing, he jogged the short distance toward his brothers as glass crunched under his feet. "Who is it, what the fuck happened?" he demanded.

Clark stood over by the bar and kicked at something. Gun smoke filled Dash's nostrils as he tried to assess what the hell happened. Bottles were in pieces on the shelves behind the bar. The mirror cracked. Someone had shot it out.

"Fucker's dead," Clark announced.

"Who?" Dash asked.

"Prospect."

"This one too," Cajun said in disgust.

"Another one over here," Mooky called from the doorway.

"I'm getting Liz the fuck out of this." Dash said. "She ain't Fury, she don't need this. She needs to be far as fuck away from this."

CHAPTER 21

Gingersnap

It only lasted a few minutes. The screams, the shots fired, the sound of things being thrown around. Now, she heard muffled music and voices. They didn't sound as urgent. Shaking, Liz stood with her ear to the bathroom door as a sense of foreboding consumed her. With two closed doors and a floor between her and whatever happened, she really couldn't hear anything of worth, but that didn't mean she'd leave the perceived safety of the bathroom.

Dash was down there. He had a meeting. He could be hurt. She was a nurse. Her shaking increased, advancing to a shiver as her mind raced. She had a professional obligation to go down there and see what happened, yet she couldn't make her feet move.

However, she was able to stretch across the floor and grab the towel she'd dropped just moments ago. Wrapping herself in the terrycloth didn't stop her shivering. The cold drops of water fell onto her shoulder from her hair, still sudsy from the shampoo. A chill ran up her spine, causing her teeth to chatter. She clutched the towel around her tighter. She needed to move.

"Liz!" Dash called from far away in a desperate tone.

"Dash!" she returned, but didn't open the door.

"Liz!" He repeated his urgent cry. The call grew louder.

"I'm here."

When the knob jiggled, she stepped back with her heart in her throat. She knew it was him. Rationally, she knew it wasn't a threat, but a small part of her questioned her ability to recognize him amid this chaos.

The door swung open. With wide, frantic eyes, her man filled the doorway before he rushed toward her. He collected her in his arms, crushing her against his chest as he ran his hand through her wet, soapy hair.

In his arms, with his protection, she let go. The sob escaped her while she wrapped her arms around him, clinging to him.

"What happened?" Her voice shook.

"Trouble," he said softly while he held her. "It's gone now."

He pulled her back and cupped her face. His gray eyes ran over her, lingering on her hair with a tight-lipped frown.

"I was in the shower." It sounded like an excuse. She didn't need one for anything, but it'd just came out that way. She sniffled as she used the back of her hand to swipe at her nose.

With a grunt, he nodded, bent at the knees, and slipped a hand against the small of her back and the other one behind her knees. They didn't speak. She let him do what he wanted. He lifted her, cradling her against his chest. As he carried Liz the few steps further into the bathroom, she hugged him, crying still.

"You stayed safe," he murmured into her hair. "That's all that matters."

When he put her down on the toilet with the lid closed, he pulled the towel from her. Cool air assaulted her and caused gooseflesh to rise over her skin. Taking her hand and placing another on the small of her back, he guided her back into the shower. As she'd never turned it off, the water continued to flow from the showerhead. Thankfully, whatever had happened downstairs hadn't been all that long because the water was still warm.

From outside the shower stall, Dash, fully clothed, reached in to work his fingers through her matted wet hair. Gently pressing into her scalp, he massaged the soap out as the water rinsed the shampoo away.

All the while she kept her eyes closed. Her mouth didn't feel as tight. Her shoulders relaxed. He must have noticed the effect he had. With a click of the cap opening and splat sound, it wasn't long before she felt the second round of shampoo applied to her hair.

"Don't go anywhere," he said when he found the towel rack empty. "I'll be right back."

Liz jerked her head, and it was back. The tight lipped frown returned. She didn't want him to leave her.

"It's right there." He gestured to the door indicating his bedroom beyond it. "I won't even leave the room."

It took a moment – as she considered it – could she risk it? Finally, she nodded.

He left the bathroom with quick steps. From her vantage point, she could see him. In the bottom drawer of his dresser, he grabbed a wash cloth. He didn't close the drawer before he trotted back to the bathroom to continue caring for his woman.

He lathered foam as he rubbed the soap against the fabric. Closing her eyes, Liz enjoyed the feel of the soft wash cloth running along her body. The tender care he used to bathe her, exploring her body in yet another way, helped the tension slowly drain from her.

This man had been exploring her, beating her, and loving her for months. He knew her. Which meant when he cleaned her, he didn't miss a spot. Had he done this any other time, she might have felt like a pampered queen.

After the second scalp massage, he walked away again. Standing under the warm spray, she watched Dash retrieve another fluffy towel from the closet. Her last one was damp. Holding open the towel, he nodded toward her. Turning off the water, she stepped out, allowing him to wrap her in the towel.

He pulled her into a protective embrace. The warmth from his strong arms further soothed her anxiety. She hadn't forgotten that something dangerous had just happened. She was very aware that the floor below them would not be how she'd last seen it. Yet, she no longer felt panic or fear.

Dash was there. He protected her. He cared for her. She nuzzled into him, not wanting to discuss it. She didn't want to have the hard conversation. Pretending it hadn't happened, that it'd all been a nightmare, would be far more convenient. Reality sucked a bag of dicks sometimes.

"We have enemies," he whispered into her hair as he rubbed her arms. "Unfortunately, they came knocking."

Swallowing the lump in her throat, she tried to keep calm. "Is everyone okay?"

The response didn't come immediately. Instead, he opted to lift her again, cradling her against him. Exiting the bathroom, he placed her on the bed. The door still closed, their privacy and security felt intact.

When he put her down, his gray eyes, far softer than she'd ever seen before, searched her features. His pain reflected at her and it choked her heart.

"No," he whispered.

"Do you need me?" she asked urgently as her nursing skills finally kicked in. If people were hurt, it was her duty to tend to them. When she tried to pull away, he clung to her, keeping her close to him.

"No," he said softly and hung his head. "I told you, I tried. I'm not a good man."

He lifted his head, his eyes, oh his eyes. Her heart broke for what she saw in his eyes.

"You've been nothing but wonderful to me." She leaned forward and cupped his face. She needed him to hear her—to see her—to understand she meant it. She wasn't just saying things.

His expression didn't change. "Get dressed. You should go home. We'll get breakfast on the way."

She wasn't prepared for what she saw. Prospects on their hands and knees scrubbed the floor. Cajun and Clark righted tables and chairs. Sarah, their normal bartender with breasts far too perky to be real, cleaned behind the counter. Her hair, she'd dyed it, but that wasn't the most alarming thing about her. No. Black stained her cheeks where her makeup had run from crying.

Someone swept up glass. "What happened?"

"Club business," he said coolly as her gaze met his. "And it's something I can't discuss. Stuff like this." He gestured to the disheveled space. "Can happen. Will happen. We try to avoid it, but it happens. I promise, with every fiber of my being, I will do my best to keep this from impacting you and keep you safe."

Business? They ran bars, clubs, and car repair shops. They had a tattoo shop. None of this made sense. And that fighting thing. Did this have to do with those fight nights?

"Did you get shot at?" she asked, noticing a hole in a couch. "Why would anyone shoot at you? You work at a bar."

Tightening his lips, he took a deep breath. The weight of something seemed to weigh him down. The responsibility, perhaps. Her gaze trailed to his vest and the patches she could see from this angle. She tried her best to process this.

"Did someone think you cheated with the fights?"

"Let's go get something to eat while they clean up."

CHAPTER 22

Dash

Dash owed her more than a McDonald's breakfast. Liz was far classier than an egg McMuffin. She deserved more. The weight of that bore down on him as he walked up the stairs to her apartment carrying the bagged breakfast.

He wasn't hungry, and he doubted she was either. Trauma did that to a person. There also was the pressing business waiting for him at the clubhouse. The surviving Roughneck Rider needed to be questioned, and he couldn't miss that. This needed to end.

At her door, he made the decision not to go inside. The time wasn't there. Either that or he didn't want to have any more conversation about things he couldn't talk about. He didn't want to lie to her. She deserved better, so much better than him.

There was also the possibility of him going in and never leaving. He couldn't risk that. Too many people counted on him returning. He promised his brothers loyalty. He couldn't leave them hanging now. No. Whiskey needed him to go back.

Liz needed him to stay. Liz needed her dominant, her man, to protect her. Fuck his conflicting priorities. This. This was why shit didn't fucking work.

Once she opened the door and stepped inside her apartment, he extended the bag toward her. He had to go. It would only be harder the longer he stayed. The puzzled expression on her face was like a knife to his chest. He had it far too bad for this woman.

"I gotta get back." He rubbed the back of his skull, knowing he sounded like a tool bag.

"Oh." She nodded, lowering her head and taking the bag. "You're not going to eat?"

She looked up at him with the question, her eyes filled with pain. Shit, this sucked and felt far too familiar. Hadn't he just done this?

"Not hungry. I'll text later?" he asked hopefully.

"Yeah," she said as the top of the bag crinkled with her curling it down. "But what happens now?"

Dash tapped his fingers on the railing. "Club—"

"I need more than that."

He took hold of his beard. "I can't."

"I was just in a place where there was a shootout. You need to."

He pinched the bridge of his nose and squeezed his eyes shut. The stress radiated through him.

"You can't just drive me home and pretend like this is just some random Tuesday."

"I know that," he snapped back.

She blinked and took a step back—startled.

He took a deep breath. "I know that," he repeated saying it softer this time. "What happens now is one of my men is going to watch over you when I can't."

"Wait what?"

"No more questions."

"What does that mean?"

"It means I have to go," he said and turned away. "Go inside. He is on his way."

"You're just going to leave?"

"Eat," he ordered, pointing to the bag. "You'll need it."

The hardest thing he'd ever done was turn his back on Liz. He'd done it fucking twice now. This time was worse. His feet felt leaden. Everything inside him screamed to stay with her, to care for her, to assure her she was safe. He'd never let anything happen to her if he could prevent it. Yet, he put her in that clubhouse knowing they were at war with an unpredictable element.

If he was going to keep Liz, and he fully intended to keep her, he needed to finish this nonsense with the Roughneck Riders. He had a vest with her name on it, literally. She was his Ol' Lady. He collared her. She was his.

He'd pussy-footed around long enough. The games were over. Lighting a cigarette, he mounted his bike. Smoke streamed from his nose on his exhale. It was the dragon's turn to play. Jackal and Tut were about to regret fucking with Dash and his brothers.

As much as Dash wanted, needed, to take a long ride on his bike, he had shit to do. The club came first. That was his vow. For the first time since he met bikers, he had something that meant more to him. Balancing, hell, sorting out how he was a dominant with a woman and a brother, no, not just a brother, being a vice president of an MC was never something he anticipated.

He'd been in it for the brotherhood, the booze, the parties, and the purpose. The money he earned doing the club's business only made his commitment that much sweeter. But now, now things were complicated. He thought he knew his shit, then she waltzed into his life and now he had to redefine everything. He had to figure it the fuck out, and soon.

Twisting the throttle harder, the bike shot forward down the road. The rush of air over him as he sped faster fueled his energy. The fucking Roughneck Rider assholes were the reason he had to deal with this shit. He'd make them pay.

THE SHED behind the clubhouse resembled a large wooden outhouse. From the outside, it looked like the place they stored their lawn care equipment. Metal gas cans sat along the outer wall, some lawnmower blades, and even an old rake.

Their newest member, Chuckie, stood at the door with his arms folded over his chest like a bouncer at a club. The intimidating look amused Dash.

"Brother." He nodded. "They start?"

Shaking his head, the recently voted in brother stepped aside. "Just came down about five minutes ago. They wanted him to sweat it out a bit."

Nodding, Dash slapped him on the shoulder and pushed the door open. The heat smacked him in the face—a dry heat that could parch a throat in seconds.

Inside the shed was a cement floor with a drain in the middle. The walls were lined with various implements meant for torture. Several ball peen hammers of various weights and sizes hung from a pegboard with clamps, hacksaws, and a few bats, both wooden and aluminum. Anyone walking into the shed wouldn't immediately assume it's true purpose —just the men had a decent amount of tools and possibly played baseball or softball or something.

The back wall had a deep, twin basin shop sink and a long

wooden workshop counter one of their brothers who worked as a carpenter had built. A single bare bulb hung from the ceiling of the windowless shed.

At the center of the room, sat a scrawny man with his sweaty head slumped forward. The only thing that kept him from face planting on the floor were the ropes wrapped around him, tying him to the chair. Dash could only assume he'd been brought there, and possibly left in the room alone while the men handled the clean-up.

Mooky stood in the back corner. A flash of white bandaging peeked from beneath the short sleeve of his t-shirt. Relief temporarily took root within Dash. His brother's injury appeared minor. Though, the ire returned because they'd injured his brother and his other brother was still with them. Whiskey needed to come home.

Cajun stood just inside the doorway, muttering under his breath as he hopped from one foot to the other. He looked like a boxer ramping up for a fight. The words he spoke were in French, so there was no hope for Dash to understand.

To Cajun's left, Clark. The president held a ball-peen hammer. He twisted the tool in his hands, almost caressing it, as if in anticipation of what was to come.

The lone survivor of their clubhouse invasion groaned and lifted his head.

"Nice of you to join us," the president said as he turned to Dash.

Dash cracked his knuckles. "Yeah, had to do something quick. Besides, with you on time, someone had to be late," he replied.

"Fuck you, fuck," the man tied to the chair spat. "I'm not fucking saying shit."

Obviously, their captive wasn't stupid. Tied to a chair, surrounded by the enemy in a dimly lit room – odds were good this wasn't a makeshift hospital. This wasn't the hospitality suite. He knew why he was there. It was a shame he planned on keeping quiet or at the very least thought he'd be keeping quiet.

They always thought that. They tried to play tough at first. Then Odin's Fury implemented their special brand of interrogation techniques and everyone sang like a canary. Every. Fucking. Time. This weasel would be no different.

The captive's swollen left eye scrunched up and blood bubbled from the split in his lip as he spoke. His brothers had given him a slight once over before taking him to the shed, which wasn't completely unexpected.

"That is not how you thank us for our hospitality," Clark commented as he swung the hammer, colliding with the young man's kneecap.

The howl that escaped the man should have been satisfying. All the Roughneck Riders needed to suffer, but this twat waffle wasn't a member. From the cut they'd taken off him, he was a damn prospect. "What kind of Mickey Mouse outfit sends prospects to invade a rival club?" Cajun said in his thick accent.

"One that ain't got no members," Mooky said.

"Roughneck Riders been around Ohio long before you and will outlive you." The young man pulled against his bonds. The chair shook with the effort.

The involuntary grin spread on Dash's face in amusement. He'd taught his brothers ties. They knew how to make them effective. One plus to being a kinky fucker.

"You are not getting out of this alive," Clark said before he slammed the hammer against the other kneecap.

The prospect screamed again as he jerked in the chair. "Fuck you," he hissed through clenched teeth.

Reaching for a long screwdriver, Dash examined it by running his finger along the length. "I don't think you are in the position to be doing any of the fucking. Now, we on the other hand—well, we can do a lot of fucking."

The man's eyes darted between Dash and Clark, each holding an implement no doubt meant to fuck his shit up. His rasping breaths came in short bursts and were the only sound in the room for now.

"You can either die a long and painful death, or we can make it quick," Clark said.

"A bullet to the temple, real quick," Mooky said as he brandished his Glock.

"Or we use every item on these walls to see how much you can bleed," Dash said, arching a brow. "My favorite color is crimson."

Cajun peered at him briefly with his word choice. Shaking it off, his club brother reached for one of the bats.

Flicking his gaze all around, their captive kept as silent as he could. There were quite a few things that would cause pain on the walls. Some blunt, some sharp. It was quite the array.

Without warning, Dash raised the screwdriver, and slammed it down into the man's thigh. The high pitched screech that followed while the man clawed at the armrests made Dash's ears ring.

"Now, you gonna tell us where you're set up, or do you want us to pull your fingernails off?" Clark asked as he dropped the hammer and reached for a pair of needle nose pliers.

CHAPTER 23

Gingersnap

*I*t may not have been her favorite food in the world, but Liz had eaten it plenty of times. However, that morning, it smelled rancid. Her stomach protested at its mere presence. The idea of putting any of what was in that bag in her mouth had her on the verge of vomiting.

Once the sound of Dash's bike had faded away, she tossed the unopened bag in the trash. Unfortunately, she could still smell the greasy breakfast inside. So, she had to. She tied off the half-filled garbage bag, and tossed it outside her apartment door.

Her neighbor slammed his car door.

The loud boom of it had her heart in her throat. It made her jump back into her place. She couldn't get the door closed fast enough. She used the weight of her entire body to shut it, but her hands shook so hard, she could barely turn the locks.

This was bad.

This was worse than Richard.

How did she let this happen?

She knew Dash was more than just a man who rode a motorcycle. She knew his leather vest – his cut – she knew it meant more than just liking a bike. That diamond patch – it meant something and she ignored it. She talked herself out of thinking about it. She let herself be enchanted, enthralled, blinded by his dominance.

Once again she let her addiction to kink get in the way of good judgement and now she was in the middle of something that had nothing to do with her. Only this time it wasn't her livelihood on the line. It wasn't just her job, her career, or her license. No. This time it wouldn't be as simple as a letter of recommendation to get her out of it. She could actually die.

There were real guns and they shot real bullets.

She upped her game this time. She'd graduated from small time criminal to mega big time felon. *What the hell was wrong with her that she couldn't find a decent human being of a man? Why couldn't she fall for a nice guy?* She seemed to sniff out and find criminals.

Wallowing in self-pity, Liz turned so her back was to the door, and slid down it. Once on her ass, she pulled her knees up close to her chest, and wrapped her arms around her legs and curled up into a ball.

She couldn't do this. She shouldn't do this. She had to stop doing this.

Liz had to end it.

She wasn't a criminal. She abided by laws. She didn't have so much as a parking ticket. How did she keep finding these men? What was it about her that attracted them?

She knew what it was about them that attracted her – their confidence – their dominance. Their control. The way they always seemed to know what to do in every situation presented to them. They never seemed rattled. They just knew shit.

She, on the other hand, felt crippled by what just happened and how this could possibly ripple and affect her. She couldn't even peel herself away from the door.

Worst of all, the only thing she wanted was Dash.

She wanted to be cuddled up with him. She wanted him to tie her up. She wanted him to blindfold her. She wanted him to take everything away so all she could concentrate on was him and what he did. She wanted to feel his control. She wanted him to make everything better. She wanted to feel his dominance because she trusted it.

It calmed her. It helped her focus. It made everything else bearable. He knew how to direct her focus. He knew how to distract her in all the right ways. She needed that now.

But she wouldn't be in this situation, she wouldn't be yearning for it this badly if it weren't for him. He was both the cause and the solution. There was no way to win in this.

As she closed her eyes, she heard the faint pops as though the gunfire she'd heard at the clubhouse were happening again but down the street from her apartment. She could smell the smoke from the freshly fired guns. Her jaw quivered. Tears streamed down her face.

Her breathing shifted from normal to husky as though she'd run a marathon. She couldn't catch her breath despite sitting there doing nothing.

Clutching her legs tighter, pulling herself in closer, trying to make herself a smaller target, she felt like her heart would explode. It beat faster and harder with each short rapid breath.

She needed Dash.
She wanted Dash.
She couldn't do this.
She shouldn't do this.

He was bad for her.

He was the reason this happened, but she still needed him to feel better.

She needed him to take all this away – to focus on something other than.

BOOM!

"Dash!" She screamed into her apartment.

Jesus Christ she was fucked up.

Sobbing, she opened her eyes. Tears blurred her vision. Slowly, her apartment came into focus, and the sounds, the smells, the panic eased.

She wasn't in the clubhouse. There were no guns. There were no other bikers who had problems with Dash and his friends.

No.

She was home. She was safe. She was in her place.

But for how long?

CHAPTER 24

Dash

*N*ástrond had four new residents. Springfield Lake served as the passage for the four unfortunate prospects tasked with storming Odin's Fury's Clubhouse and couldn't get away. There had to have been more. No way only four dickwads could have pulled it off. They were practically kids, barely out of high school. Dash doubted they could even legally drink. Unfortunately, their actions had consequences. Can't do adult things without adult ramifications. For Dash, it was another reason to gut Jackal and Tut. Fucking cowards couldn't even do it themselves.

Dumping a body was a lot of work. Dumping four sucked. Their most established prospects, one in his late twenties and the other in his early thirties, were tasked with the responsibility. Odin's Fury didn't deal with teenagers. Once the bodies were dismembered, the two men went on their way and the newer prospects were tasked with cleaning the shed.

Four days had passed since the attack on their clubhouse.

The hang arounds and most of the club sluts weren't phased. He doubted most of the hang arounds knew or cared. The brothers were around more, protecting what was theirs, and expectantly more vigilant. Everyone was on edge, ready to put this to bed. Tonight they'd do that.

Mittens and Romeo arrived last night as a sign of Monty's support. Not that he didn't think they could handle it; he knew they could. He wanted there to be no question that the national chapter wouldn't stand for disrespect from the local chapters. The message was heard loud and clear. It helped boost the sense of brotherhood and loyalty within their ranks. Someone had their back, they weren't acting alone. He suspected the former Roughneck Riders, having been a significantly smaller club, hadn't had that sort of support before.

Riding in the cage, a conversion van they'd obtained for purposes such as this, added to Dash's annoyance with the situation. When with his brothers, he preferred the wind to being cooped up. Cages had their place. It wasn't when he was with his brothers.

Tapping his finger on the steering wheel to the beat of *Jekyll and Hyde* by Five Finger Death Punch got his adrenaline pumping. He wanted to be amped up and ready to end this. The sooner it ended, the sooner Whiskey could come home, the sooner things could go back to normal, and he'd figure shit out with Liz.

Liz.

Their texts had been brief, almost cold. Being at the club-house when it got invaded by asshats had changed things with her. He should have expected that. Everyone had limits. Not every man was made to wear a diamond 1% patch. Not every woman could handle being with the type of man who earned one.

It didn't make his desire for Liz any less. It didn't make

his need for her wane. Liz was his, goddamnit. He'd fucking protect her. He should have done a better job of it. He'd gotten sloppy and now things had changed.

Their messages weren't as flirty. The vibe was off. Though, he tried to convince himself, his distraction had more to do with it than her. For her, he assumed, she was still rattled. He couldn't blame her. She may not be the kind of woman who could handle the life of a one percenter yet, but he wanted her to be. He ached for her to be, needed her to be that kind of woman. He could help her get there, if she let him.

The only way to get back to her, to figure out what the hell they were doing together, was to end this shit with the Roughneck Riders. They *all* needed to go to Nástrǫnd. So, he had to get his game face on. The dragon needed to take over. Gritting his teeth, he bopped his head to the rough guitar and speed drumming. Nástrǫnd would be crowded tonight.

The new Roughneck Riders' clubhouse was a dilapidated warehouse with cracked crumbling concrete walls. A single chain link fence surrounded the overgrowth covering the distance of the perimeter of the building. When he pulled the van over to park at the corner of the property, Dash studied the structure. He noted they hadn't even installed security cameras.

"Fucking idiots," he muttered. A decent sized lot housed a few bikes and a few cars lit by two flood lights mounted to the front wall. At midnight, a few people milled around outside, no doubt they had a party going.

His eye twitched at the idea of citizens being there and getting caught in the crossfire. He could write them off as trash for going to the Roughneck Riders instead of Odin's Fury, but he doubted they knew better. For most, a party was a party. They didn't know shit about shit.

Dash, Romeo, Mittens, and Cajun exited the van dressed

head to toe in dark camouflage with face paint. AR-15s with the serial numbers filed off hung from their backs. They didn't come to play. The Roughneck Riders would get a final lesson tonight in MC life.

Using the dark night as cover, they scouted the place. Crouch walking through the tall, unkempt grass worked to their advantage as they fanned out and slowly approached the clubhouse. Recalling his military training, they used hand signals instead of speaking or radios to keep quiet. The plan was to surprise them.

In the short time they'd known of the location, they'd only been able to accomplish limited reconnaissance work. The building had one door in the front of the warehouse and three trucking bays in the back.

They wanted all the angles covered. Their plan had Cajun and Mittens in the back. Dash and Romeo were to cover the front door. Doing their best to keep out of sight, they watched the comings and goings as they hid behind cars in the parking lot. Biding their time was imperative to ensure they spared as many civilians as they could. Casualties were reserved only for any wearing a Riders cut.

The pocket of Dash's black cargo pants vibrated. Since they were officially out of line of sight, they had to rely on other means of communication. Only Cajun had the number. Without answering it, he pulled it from his pocket, showed it to Romeo. Once he got the nod from his brother, he rose to his feet, and stomped on it.

Cajun and Mittens were in position. Slinging their guns forward, Dash gave one more nod to Romeo. It was go time. He and his brother let out a battle cry as they charged toward the front door.

"Get the fuck out of here!" They screamed at the few people outside who shrieked while they scrambled away at the sight and sound of the men of Odin's Fury.

Before the portly prospect at the door could pull his gun, Dash fired. His target's arms flailed outward as his body flew back against the exterior wall of the clubhouse. Romeo kicked the door in.

"Get the fuck out! Party is fucking over!" Dash bellowed, firing into the ceiling before the back doors opened with Cajun and Mittens joining them.

Chaos ensued. A crowd charged toward them amid shouts of panic.

Doing his best to dodge them, Dash kept his eye on the bar. A Roughneck Rider cut caught his eye. He aimed. Pulling the trigger sent the gun recoiling into his shoulder repeatedly as a series of bullets hit his intended target.

A screaming bystander collided with him, tripping. Dash's arms shifted and his bullets went slightly left of where he'd aimed. His finger relaxed off the trigger as the citizen fell to the ground beside him.

Glaring down, but not truly seeing who it was—only that the individual did not possess a cut of any sort, he snarled. "Get the fuck out of here or get hurt."

Romeo's gun went off again, but Dash didn't have time to note his brother's progress. Moving against the tide, he shoved the panicked party goers out of the way when more gunfire, not AR-15 gunfire, joined the fight.

The crowd thinned in moments with so many exits. Taking cover behind an overturned table, Dash shot back at the sound of the gunfire. When he peeked over the table, his shoulder felt as though it exploded. Blood splashed against his cheek, his own blood.

He ducked back behind the table and rolled to an upended couch. He didn't have time to do a thorough inspection, but he tried to do what he could quickly. Testing his range of motion caused excruciating pain, but he could still move, which meant he could still shoot.

On his belly, he wriggled under the flying bullets, looking for more targets. *Pop pop pop.* He pulled the trigger at the sight of scuffed motorcycle boots, causing the man in them to topple to the ground.

Minutes.

The exchange was over in mere minutes. Gun fights weren't long affairs in real life. Movies dramatized them. They could take a half an hour, but Dash had never been in one that lasted more than a few minutes.

"Romeo," he shouted as the bullets died down.

"All good, VP," his brother hollered back.

"Cajun," Dash checked in.

"Clear, *cher*," He drawled back from somewhere.

"Mittens." The last call was for their Eastern-Bloc boxer.

"Bloody, but I've seen worse."

With all his men accounted for, Dash slowly rose, letting the gun clatter to the floor. He scanned the room, searching for signs of life. A few people cowered under tables, crying.

"Get the fuck out of here." Cajun's thick accent made the demand that much more heinous.

"Fan out. Do a check," Dash ordered. He didn't want any fucking surprises. He also needed to find Whiskey. "Cops should be here soon."

"Nine minutes out," Mittens informed.

They had, at most, five minutes to find Whiskey. Once they had him, they'd have to get to the van and get out of there before the cops showed up. Before that, they had to set up the clubhouse for a police raid.

"Someone got Tut," Romeo called out as he shoved a body around. "Fucker."

Dash nodded at the disappointment in his brother's tone and turned down a hallway. No doubt his brothers wanted him to suffer for his life choices. Some things couldn't be helped.

"Fuck you!" The pained cry rose higher than the soft rock music still playing from somewhere.

"Jackal's still kicking," Cajun boomed, causing Dash to stop mid-step. His brothers had a chance to take out their fury on him.

"This isn't over. Riders forever. Forever Rid—ugh." The grunt interrupting his words gave Dash a sense of satisfaction. They weren't just ending the poor excuse for an MC, but their rhetoric as well.

"Where's Whiskey?" Romeo demanded from the other room.

The request made Dash grin. He doubted Jackal knew the road name Whiskey used. However, the fact they hadn't found him yet, or that he hadn't come out after the gunfire, meant the shit's more than likely figured him out.

The thought turned Dash's blood cold. He needed to find his brother.

"Booze is behind the bar," Jackal wheezed.

The sound of fist hitting flesh was a mix between a squishy sound and a slap when the punch drew blood. Hearing it meant Romeo had done just that.

"Your fucking plant?" Jackal's pained laugh pierced Dash, despite its abrupt stop when he figured Romeo had shut him up.

"Torch him," Dash said when he came face to face with a room padlocked to shit on the outside. Whatever was behind that door was important.

"Three minutes, VP." Mittens appeared at his back.

Dash jutted his chin at the door. "Their stash?" he guessed.

"Doubt it." Mittens stepped around him and fingered the locks. "Found a fuck ton of shit in the office."

Clenching his jaw, the acting vice president of Odin's

Fury Ohio's chapter stared at the door. "What do we have to bust it down?"

Mittens tapped on the door and tested the knob. "I got an idea."

Smoke wafted toward him, accompanied by pained screams. Justice welled in him. The threat of the Roughneck Riders burned in that room and would no longer bother Odin's Fury. However, the good feeling was short-lived.

The door stood between him and the answer as to where Whiskey could be. He reared back and did his best kick. In the movies, doors gave way with a simple kick. Not so much in real life. Dash had mentioned those biker shows exaggerated things. He was now face to face with that fact. Or, well, foot to face. Pain vibrated up his leg, lingering at his knee. He hissed as he bounced off it.

The door remained on its hinges, though cracked, and taunted him. Muttering curses at himself, he rubbed at his kneecap. If Whiskey wasn't in that room, he didn't know where else to look. They didn't have time to continue the search.

"Two minutes, fifteen seconds." Mittens came back with a crowbar.

It took some doing. With a bit of leverage, the two of them broke the padlocks. The wood of the door splintered as they worked the crowbar between the jamb and the knob. The barrier gave way. With the pressure of the clock ticking in his head, the pair burst through the entryway. Relief washed over him.

Unconscious, lying on the bloodstained ground, was their brother Whiskey. He was in terrible shape. Quickly, Dash knelt at his side and checked his vitals. The beat of his pulse against Dash's fingers was the most wonderful feeling he'd ever had, even as weak as it was—the fact it existed was all that mattered.

Hoisting him up, Dash positioned his brother across his shoulders. Using the firefighter's carry for Whiskey, he turned to Mittens. "Let's get the fuck out of here." Mitten's high-pitched whistle followed. The five members of Odin's Fury ran out the back doors of the clubhouse and through the overgrowth. By the time they got to their van, sirens grew louder. They missed them by twenty seconds, passing them on the road as they headed back to Akron and their own clubhouse.

CHAPTER 25

Gingersnap

*L*iz had called out of work. She'd blown off Ane and Pup when they texted. Even the few texts she'd exchanged with Dash were superficial. Sitting on her couch, she wore the same pajama pants and tank top she'd put on the night Dash left her at her apartment. She hadn't left the couch cushion since he'd left.

Reruns of *Scrubs* played on the TV, but it didn't register. She didn't even know what season or episode played. She didn't watch. She hadn't slept over fifteen minutes since he left. Everything became a blur.

Every time she started falling asleep, she'd hear it again. Pops of gunfire. The shaking of the building, the screaming. She'd jolt upright, heart racing, and it'd take her a second or so to realize she wasn't in the clubhouse. She was home. She was safe, but she didn't feel it.

The knock at the door startled her. Truth be told, she'd expected it. It made no sense that it had scared her. Taking a deep breath, she brought her hands over her face. She didn't have the energy to deal with her friends right now. She just wanted to be left alone to manage this. Not that she knew what 'this' was or what it would mean, but she needed to sort out her feelings and her life.

However, her friends weren't the type to just go away. They were good like that. Reluctantly, she dragged herself off the couch and unlocked her door. They wouldn't go away. If they'd started showing up at her place unannounced, they wouldn't leave if she told them. They were far better friends than that, for which she was thankful. Opening the door, she braced herself for the verbal assault from them.

On the other side, the wild haired, green-eyed, freckle-faced woman smiled at her. The warm smile, the casual stance, and the apologetic look in her eyes befuddled Liz.

"Hi." Sparrow offered with a small wave. "I thought we could talk."

Self-consciously, Liz reached up for the messy knot she'd put in her hair to keep it out of her face.

"Sure." She stepped back, allowing the woman into her place.

"I've been wanting to call you, but Dash doesn't seem to want to give out your number," Sparrow said as her gaze drifted around Liz's apartment.

Passing her guest, Liz attempted to clean up the mess in her living room. Seeing her place through the other woman's eyes embarrassed her.

"You could've asked me," she said as she crunched up an empty bag of chips and collected a few water bottles. "You want something to drink?"

Sparrow took a seat on the couch. "You got beer?"

"I think so," she said as she went into the kitchen.

"I love this show." Her guest pointed to the screen.

"Huh?" Liz had forgotten what was on the TV. She glanced at the screen. "Oh." She blushed slightly, realizing how out-of-sorts she was and how bad she must look. "Yeah. It's a classic."

Retrieving two bottles of beer from the refrigerator, she twisted off the caps, and headed back to the couch with one outstretched for Sparrow. She couldn't let the woman drink alone. It was a woman's code.

"Thanks," Sparrow said before she took a sip. Her gaze followed Liz as she took a seat opposite her on the couch. With a quick flick of the remote, Sparrow turned the TV off, allowing silence to fill the space.

The two women watched one another. Liz became very aware of how she looked, but leaving the woman alone while she put herself together seemed far ruder than remaining in her multi-day-worn, stained jammies. She hadn't showered either, and probably had a bit of a smell to her. *What a mess.*

"How you doing?" Sparrow asked.

With an arched brow, Liz didn't answer.

An understanding smile spread on the biker's girlfriend's face. "Yeah." She nodded. "Sometimes we all forget that it's not normal."

"That's normal?" Liz asked in disbelief as she gestured her beer toward the window as though the clubhouse were just on the other side of it.

Somehow, Sparrow chortled. How she could be smiling, hell in a good mood, after what happened in the clubhouse, confused Liz.

"No," she admitted with her head down. "Not really, but I guess we are more prepared because it's happened before." She shrugged, bringing her head up. "It's not that we expect it. It's not a goal or anything, but we know it's a possibility. I guess Dash didn't really prepare you for that."

Frowning, Liz glanced out the window. The look in the other woman's eyes felt like a toss-up between pity and empathy. There was a thin line between the two. Liz had used that look far too many times at work when taking care of terminal patients. Seeing it on someone else's face, directed toward her, made the lost feeling worse. "I guess not."

The heat of Sparrow's hand on her thigh caused Liz to jerk her head back to the woman. Instead of meeting her gaze, though, Liz peered down at the hand on her thigh. The gesture had to be meant for comfort, but it made her that much more uneasy.

"He's a good guy," Sparrow offered. "He doesn't want to hurt you."

Slowly, Liz pulled her gaze up to her guest's face. The hand retreated and with it went the anxiety she'd felt.

"He loves you," she said. "A guy doesn't make a woman his Ol' Lady for nothing, you know. That means something."

Liz's brows flew up. He hadn't mentioned anything about being an Ol' Lady. When she scanned Sparrow, she noted the vest wasn't there. Every Ol' Lady wore a vest when around the club proclaiming to whom she belonged. Yet her visitor hadn't worn it that night.

"He didn't tell you," she surmised with a tight-lipped grin. The beer bottle tilted up as Sparrow took another swallow.

Nope. He hadn't told her shit. She wasn't even sure how something like that happened. *What did it even mean other than she got to ride on the back of his bike?*

"Sorry." A shrug accompanied the apology.

Of all the things that had gone down, not telling her about being Dash's Ol' Lady was the least of her concerns. This woman needed some perspective.

"He should've been the one to tell you. Act surprised when he does." She offered a nervous laugh. "I was born into this. My dad was the Sergeant at Arms here. I don't know any other life than this," she said before chewing on her bottom lip as she studied Liz.

Liz shook her head slightly. This is what happened when someone got accustomed to the life of being with a biker. She let out a low huff. They got used to being near shoot outs. They brushed them off like they were nothing. She wasn't sure she could handle that.

"It's not for everyone. I've seen bitches come and go out of the club. I've seen *guys* come and go because *they* can't hack it. It's fucking hard."

"On that we agree," Liz mumbled.

Taking a deep breath, Sparrow focused on the label on her bottle. She pursed her lips as she peeled at it.

Taking a big swallow of beer, Liz wished for wine. If only Ane were there to hug her and support her through this. She didn't know how to feel or deal with this. She hadn't processed a damn thing.

"My dad died in something like that," Sparrow admitted before looking up. "As far as I know, that was the last time the clubhouse got hit."

"Jesus," Liz hissed, and now she wanted to comfort the other woman. She reached for Sparrow's hand.

With half a smile, Sparrow accepted the hand holding and offered Liz's hand a squeeze. "My parents knew what they were going into." She shrugged. "I think adjusting to my dad dying was harder than processing how it happened."

Nodding, Liz didn't interrupt or argue. She'd seen that while working hospice. When the loved one finally passed, it was almost a relief to the family.

"It's not the norm. That was years ago." Sparrow offered another hand squeeze.

"But it happens," Liz challenged.

"Not enough for it to be a real worry."

"He could die." The words left Liz and strangled her. Her heart tightened, and she wanted to take it back. She didn't want to think about that, about losing him on that level.

Losing him as a boyfriend, as a dominant, was one thing, but losing him from existence was an entirely different kettle of fish. She didn't think she could actually handle that—not that she was handling this very well.

"He could die in a bike wreck," Sparrow countered without missing a beat. "Does that mean he shouldn't ride?"

Dash loved to ride, and she loved to ride with him. The bike was just as addicting as the man. "That's different."

"It's not really." Sparrow took another swallow of beer. "We are temporary. Our existence in this world, we're not meant to be here forever. We're given a finite amount of time to be on this Earth and to live. The way I look at it, I've got about a good sixty years left to enjoy all that life has to offer, the good and the bad. The bad strengthens us, the good makes it worth it. I won't miss out on love because of fear. It's just not something I'm willing to give up."

Two huge gulps of beer slid down Liz's throat. At a loss for what to do with the conversation, she lowered her gaze, scanning the label of her own bottle for answers. She wasn't prepared for this existential discussion.

"All I'm saying is that I don't let fear rule me." Sparrow put her beer down on the floor and used both her hands to hold Liz's one.

Liz looked up to meet the woman's gaze.

"I got one life to live. Jacob, uh." She chuckled, her cheeks flushed with a bit of a blush. "Romeo." She corrected with a sly smile.

Jacob. His real name was Jacob. The idea that this woman freely used his legal name caught Liz off guard, and she didn't quite understand why.

"Romeo is worth the risk," Sparrow said.

Liz inhaled audibly as she considered Dash and all he was to her, how he treated her, and everything their relationship had been. She thought of how he made her feel like the absolute center of the world.

"I'd miss out on so much love and goodness if I let fear chase me away from Romeo." She licked her bottom lip, but held Liz's gaze. "The club…the club is my family. I'm scared as fuck when they go on runs and do jobs, but that's the life. Every family has its good, and it's bad. Mine is just more intense. The highs are fucking high." She grinned.

Liz couldn't help but think of the highs Dash awarded her when he took her deep into subspace. No one got her there like he did.

"The lows, well." She sighed heavily. "Are pretty fucking low, but we use that to motivate us and give us strength."

Liz lowered her gaze to her hand, held in Sparrow's two. The weight of all this bore down on her and she just wanted to take a nap. She wanted to sleep for three days, for a week, for a month. She didn't want to have to deal with this. Turning back time, to before this happened, to the first scene with Dash, was far more desirable than where they were now.

"You don't have to make a decision now." Sparrow shook their joined hands before releasing them. "Just think about it. He's a good fucking man who does bad things for his family. He loves you."

Love. That word jarred Liz, causing her to blink and gape at Sparrow. They hadn't used that word with one another, yet her guest flaunted it nonchalantly, like it was some well-known fact. Clearing her throat, Liz shook it off. Far too much at once. Feeling overwhelmed, she decided to just focus on the present and Sparrow.

Her guest pushed off the couch to stand.

Putting her own beer down, Liz did the same.

"I'm going to head out." Sparrow gestured with her thumb over her shoulder. "You have to process all this. I just wanted you to know." She paused, stuffing her hands in her pockets, lifting her shoulders up. "I just wanted you to know the facts."

Liz nodded and was caught off guard when Sparrow's arms came around her. The squeeze made her return the hug. She needed it. She needed the reassurance. Ane and Pup, they'd hug her, they'd be there for her, but in the end, they didn't know. Sparrow knew.

Breaking the hug, Sparrow stepped back and held her arms as she looked in her eyes. "You aren't in this alone. I'm not talking about Dash. Me. Call me sometime. We can talk about it." She handed Liz a slip of paper with her number written on it and winked.

CHAPTER 26

Dash

*C*ajun drove the van back to the clubhouse. Mittens faced the rear while Dash checked Whiskey over. Romeo sat on an inner wheel well hump watching, waiting to be of assistance. So far, all Dash had given him to do was hold Whiskey's clothes that they'd stripped off him before examining his injuries.

"Breathing is good," Dash called out to no one in particular. He placed his ear to his chest and listened to the *thump bump* of his heart beat. "Heart is ticking."

"He looks really bad," Romeo said with his gaze locked on their brother's features.

The swelling in his face made assessing it harder, though Dash thought it safe to assume he had, at the very least, a broken nose and possibly an orbital fracture of his right eye. As he trailed his fingers around Whiskey's forehead, his temples, and the back of his head, nothing more than swelling gave an indication of a more serious injury.

"The club needs to invest in an X-ray machine," he

mumbled to himself, knowing that it was highly unlikely and not exactly feasible.

"Can you get those?" Romeo asked, and it reminded Dash of just how young his protégée was.

"You can get anythin' if you try hard enough," Cajun drawled from the front seat. "Don't mean it's smart."

Further assessing Whiskey, Dash tuned out his brothers as they discussed the logistics of an X-ray machine for the clubhouse. Neck seemed okay. Shoulders, arms, and then his fingers. A bunch of them were snapped, and getting them splinted would be all he could offer. His brother had to be in extreme pain.

As the van turned, he braced himself before trying to assess his chest. Even in his unconscious state, he winced when Dash touched his side. It drew Romeo's attention. "He waking up?"

"I hope not," Dash admitted. "He'll be in a fuck ton of pain." There was no way around that. Just from the injuries he'd assessed, his brother had to suffer.

"I don't like him being out like that," Mittens commented. "The longer he's out the worse it is." As a fighter, Mittens had a pretty decent perspective on this.

"We don't have anything to give him for pain," Dash said as he moved down. The bruising on Whiskey's side worried him. It could be a sign of internal bleeding. No doubt the cowards had kicked him when he was down.

"Then we can get some," Romeo declared.

"He needs more than Tylenol," Dash said as he looked over Whiskey's legs. "Heavy duty shit. We can't get that at the pharmacy with our good looks."

"Isn't Ginger a nurse?" his younger brother asked. "Sparrow said something about her being a nurse."

"No." Dash cut that line of thinking off. Things were weird between them, and he didn't want to drag her into anything more deeply than he already had.

"She a nurse, *cher?*" Cajun asked over his shoulder at a stop light.

"Look at him, man." Romeo gestured as though Dash hadn't noticed Whiskey lying on the floor of the van between them, moaning.

Shaking his head, Dash sat back on his heels. "No."

"Maybe she could get what we need from the hospital," Mittens chimed in.

"I said fucking no," Dash barked as he looked over his unconscious brother. "She doesn't work at a hospital, anyway," he added a bit more calmly. "She's not that kind of nurse. She's a visiting nurse. The kind that goes to people's houses."

He was out of his depth. Whiskey needed more care than an old field medic could provide. He needed a better exam. Fuck, his brother needed a damn doctor. Scrubbing his hand over his bald head, he struggled with his loyalties. His club came first and his woman second. This was club life. He knew this.

Letting out a groan of frustration, he thudded his fist against his chest. He wasn't double jointed enough to thump against the colors on his back, but that was the sentiment. He'd never expected to be in this sort of position. Serious relationships weren't his thing. This was a perfect reason to avoid them.

Thankfully, his brothers said nothing more during the ride back. They didn't even have the radio on. He'd kill for some music to focus on. Then again, it would distract him from listening to the wheezing breaths coming from Whiskey.

They pulled into the clubhouse compound and drove around to the back. As carefully as they could, Dash and Romeo carried an unconscious, grunting Whiskey into the clubhouse and to a bedroom. Clark was inside waiting for them.

"Shit," he hissed the moment he spotted Whiskey. "How bad is it?"

"Don't know," Dash admitted as he dragged his hand down his beard. Curling his fingers around the length, he tugged. The inner battle whether to call Liz waged on in his head.

Nodding, Clark took out his phone. "I'll let Monty know. Doesn't he have a doctor, something on payroll?"

"In Montana." Mittens with his gaze locked on the man in the bed.

"I need to get one of those," Clark said before greeting Monty on the phone. He exited the room to talk.

When Whiskey coughed and tried to roll, his eyes fluttered, trying to open. Dash quickly kneeled at his side. "We got you, brother," he said, trying to sound sure of himself. "You're out of there. We got you out."

More coughing and winces were his response.

"He needs a doctor." Romeo's nerves broke through his speech.

All of them had been around beaten men before. Usually, they were the ones causing the beating. Typically, there was a sense of satisfaction when a man was in this state, but this was different. Their brother laid there. They hadn't done it. This was their brother, and they needed to fix it.

"I'll call her." Dash hung his head in resignation.

CHAPTER 27

Liz

Staring at the television, not watching it, but just zoning out in that direction, Liz didn't recognize her cell ringing. The sound registered, but she didn't connect that it was hers. Finally, it made sense. Blinking, she came out of her daze and searched for her phone.

When she grabbed it, a photo of her and Dash appeared on her screen.

"Hey," she answered. She didn't know how she felt about all this, but she knew she didn't want to ignore him. Things may be weird, but he'd made an effort to check in for the past four days.

"I'm sending a prospect to get you." He skipped the pleasantries.

"What?" She sat up. *Get her?* "Where am I going?"

She looked around the room as though one of his club brothers would appear out of nowhere.

"Why? I haven't even showered." *In days.* The words fell

out of her mouth as she stood up and used her free hand to run through some knots in her hair.

"The clubhouse. You have ten minutes," Dash replied curtly. "Quick shower. Bring your medical bag."

"What? Why?"

Click.

"Dash?" She knew the sound of a hang up, but maybe she heard wrong.

"Dash?" she repeated before she pulled the phone from her face and saw the time flash one last time before it went to her lock screen.

Confused, she stared at the phone, willing him to call back. Hell, send a text. She'd accept a smoke signal at this point. Unsure what else to do, she headed toward the bathroom, leaving her phone on the counter. If she was to be seen, she had better not stink like Cheetos and body odor.

While fastening the button to her jeans with a damp head of hair, the knock at the door startled her.

"Coming!" she said as she grabbed a t-shirt from her dresser. "I'm coming," she repeated, making her way through her apartment, pulling the shirt over her head.

Droplets of water flicked around as she ran her fingers through her wet hair. She hadn't even had time to blow dry it before the prospect arrived. When she opened the door, she didn't expect who stood there. "Ane."

"We drew straws," she said, pushing past Liz. "We figured if we both came at you, it might be overwhelming. So, lucky me." She sounded sarcastic.

Closing the door, Liz chewed on the bottom of her lip. She didn't know what was going on, but the prospect would arrive soon.

"I have to say I did expect you in worse shape," her friend said. "The fact that you've showered is a good sign."

"I'm actually on my way out the door."

Ane drew her brows together. "We figured that's where you disappeared to." She folded her arms over her chest. "You could have told me."

"I did tell you," Liz countered as she looked for her shoes. Flip-flops would be best. No need for socks. But, wait. She might need them. "I texted when I left. I just didn't tell you where I went."

"Bitch," Ane snapped, drawing Liz's focus. "Seriously, after everything you two went through, you just jumped when he snapped his fingers? This is classic want what you can't have."

Heading down the hallway, she had to get socks. If the biker coming to get her had his bike, well, then she couldn't wear flip-flops. They'd be convenient in the moment, but in the long run, she'd probably lose a toe.

"It's not like that," Liz said far too distracted by the idea she had but seconds before the prospect came.

"Where are you going? Is he coming now? If so, I have some words for him." Her friend followed behind her.

Socks in hand, Liz got on all fours and searched for her sneakers under the bed. "You don't have to have words," she said as she pulled out one shoe and then the other.

"It's a best friend thing," Ane replied with her hands on her hips. "I'm protective."

Smiling, Liz pulled on her socks while sitting on the floor with her back to the bed. "I love you and truly don't deserve you. I don't know what's going on, honestly. We didn't really talk."

Ane arched her brow.

"Don't look at me like that. He's good," she said as she stuffed one foot in her shoe and then the other. "I don't know what I want, let alone what he wants."

"You're wearing his collar," Ane pointed out.

Liz's hand went up, and she fingered the metal ring around her neck. She'd grown accustomed to the weight of it and had forgotten it was there. It brought her comfort even in the haze the past few days had become.

"Yeah. You know what you want," Ane said and stepped into the room, wrapping her arms around Liz. "Just promise me you won't let him hurt you again, okay?"

Liz gave her friend a good squeeze. "I won't." A promise she knew she couldn't keep. She'd fallen so hard for Dash, there was no way he'd not hurt her.

The knock at her door interrupted their moment. She pulled away from Ane and nodded. "I won't," she assured her friend before stepping away. "Coming."

Phone in the pocket. Medical bag over her shoulder. Best friend at her heels. This would be a night for sure. "What do you need that for?" Ane asked from behind her.

Instead of answering, she opened the door to find an anxious young biker facing her. "Ginger?" he asked as he stuffed his hands in his front pockets.

"Yeah." She nodded.

Ane sidled up beside her and eyed the young guy as though he were her prom date with a reputation. "I know all the pressure points and took seven years of Ju Jitsu."

"What?" the poor biker asked as he shifted from foot to foot.

Liz rolled her eyes. "Ignore her."

The three walked down the stairs in silence. Shifting the bag on her shoulder, she said goodbye to Ane at the foot of the stairs and turned to the man with 'prospect' patched on the back of his cut. She scanned the lot for a bike. "So what do you ride?" she asked. "Do you have saddlebags? I'm not sure my bag will fit."

"Got a cage," he said as he led her to a pickup truck.

"Oh." She nodded slightly, disappointed that she wouldn't be on a bike.

"You think Dash would let anyone put his woman on the back of their bike?" he scoffed. "Crazy woman."

CHAPTER 28

Dash

*S*he showed up to the clubhouse in skinny jeans that hugged every curve she had with a cute, vintage, lemon lime t-shirt, and her medical bag slung over her shoulder. The collar around her neck made his chest twinge. Dash's collar. She still wore it after he'd put it on her the other night.

It took only a few steps to close the distance between them from the foot of the bed. His arms found her and pulled her against his chest as though of their own accord. If he'd wanted to show restraint, he'd lost that battle. Taking a deep inhale of her hair, he knew he'd never want to go another day without it.

"I'm sorry," he whispered. He'd bring her deep down into a world she didn't belong. She was far too good for his world, for him. His selfishness wouldn't allow him to let her go again. He tried. It didn't take.

"For what?" she asked before she let out a gasp. "My god!" She pulled out of his arms.

Reluctantly, Dash let her go. Rubbing his hand along the back of his head, he fought the urge to continue to touch her.

"His injuries are beyond my skill set."

With a slack jaw, Liz put her bag down and looked over at the man in the bed. "Who is he?" she asked, glancing over her shoulder.

"Whiskey Tango Foxtrot," Romeo answered. "We call him Whiskey, though."

"A brother in a bad way. I didn't want to call you, but—" Dash held out his hands, palms up pathetically. He'd never felt so ill-equipped before.

She nodded. "I'll do what I can," she assured him and rubbed his arm before rifling through her bag. "I don't have a lot of things."

She pulled her stethoscope out first and hung it around her neck. Then she grabbed saline flushes, a blood pressure cuff, sterilized gauze, some over the counter pain medications, and gloves. The gloves snapped when she pulled them on. Watching his woman slip into her professional mode was like watching a switch flip.

Her focus zeroed in on Whiskey like the rest of the men in the room weren't there. She moved around him, checking vitals, taking his blood pressure, and cleaning out wounds. As she worked, the bloody, gruesome face he'd stared into the last hour looked less fatal. His hope for his brother to pull through was raised because of his woman.

"There's no way for me to know the extent of his injuries," she said while placing a gauze pad near the split in his cheek.

"We just need to know if he's going to live," Clark responded somberly.

"Can you use these?" Cajun asked as he held up some of the left over things from when Bowie had been in hospice. Unused liquid morphine, saline bags, and some antibiotics.

Liz's eyes brightened at their arrival. "Where did you get these?" she asked as she took them, checking them over. "They're not expired. I think it could help. Way better than the over the counter stuff I have."

Cajun grinned, the obvious pride on his face. "I have ways."

"But legally…" she trailed off.

"It might be best not to ask certain questions," Dash said.

"Get the rest of the stuff from Bowie," Clark ordered no one in particular. Several men took off to follow the directive.

"Our president died of cancer," Mooky said from the corner of the room. "We never got around to returning the stuff from when he was here."

Liz looked over her shoulder at Dash. He didn't have to tell her. They didn't need words. He merely nodded to let her know that yes, the funeral she'd attended had been the source of the medication she now had.

She licked her bottom lip and turned back to her patient. Whiskey was in solid hands. His woman would make him better. Bringing his hands together, Dash closed his eyes and thanked all that was holy for her coming into his life. There were a thousand reasons to be grateful, but right now, the one that mattered was that she'd save his brother. That was a debt he'd never be able to repay, but he vowed then and there, he'd die trying.

Gingersnap

AFTER TWO HOURS, Liz was satisfied she'd done all she could for Whiskey. Whoever had beaten him, because there was no way around it, he'd been beaten, did a thorough job. She was pretty sure there was a boot print on his back. With the IV line set, antibiotics in his system, and even the pain medicine, she was sure his comfort had increased significantly since before she arrived.

She ordered everyone out of his room. Mittens, the square-jawed boxer, was the only one who refused her demand. With his arm around her shoulder, Dash assured her, Mittens wouldn't disturb her patient.

After closing the door, leaving the two men inside, Liz faced her man. With the crisis now handled, or as handled as it could be without a hospital, she looked up at him. His hands held her waist protectively as he kissed her forehead.

"What happened to him?" she asked, unsure if he would actually give her an answer.

He pressed his forehead to hers. After a moment, he rocked it back and forth. "We can't talk here. Let's go to my room."

He took deep inhale before he broke free. His hand sought hers. With a squeeze, he led her down the hall toward the room he called his. The door closed, and he gestured to the bed for her to sit.

She figured that the more she complied with him, the more likely he would be to tell her what she wanted to know. Though, she wasn't sure she wanted to know much. Maybe the television show wasn't an exaggeration.

"I can't say much or give you too many details and, baby, I don't want to lie to you." He sounded vulnerable, so much so her heart pinched.

"Then don't," she croaked as emotion balled in her throat.

"I won't, but you have to promise me, if I tell you that stuff is club business, you leave it alone." He knelt down before her and rested his hands on her thighs. The look in his gray eyes, his expression, was not what she expected.

Normally he had confidence about him. He carried

himself with effortless pride and command of the room. Kneeling in front of her, looking at her with large puppy dog eyes and a voice thick with emotion, he was anything but proud or confident.

"I promise," she assured him as she ran her hand along his cheek, desperate for another expression.

"Another club had a beef with ours." Dash took a deep breath. "It took far longer than expected to put it to bed. It's done." He squeezed her thighs. "I promise you, it's done." He inched closer and rested his head on her thighs. "I nearly lost my brother today. You brought him back to me. Please, don't make me lose my woman."

Tears welled in her eyes at his words. The ball in her throat choked her. She ran her hand over the stubble of his head. "You aren't losing me," she whispered and slid down the end of the bed.

The two of them knelt before one another, meeting each other's tear-filled eyes. She wrapped her arms around him and held him tight. He encircled her waist to return the embrace. They exchanged squeezes before he guided her up to her feet.

She closed her eyes at the feel of warmth on her neck. His kisses trailed toward her collarbone as his hands slid up her sides and then back down to her ass. She moaned as he pulled her harder, grinding her against him.

With a groan, his teeth grazed her skin. "Mine," he whispered. "All mine."

"Yours," she agreed.

When his fingers trailed up her sides, the tingles tickled her. She squirmed, wriggling, and bit her bottom lip, trying not to let the giggles escape. His index finger curled around the thick ring circling her throat, making it tighter. "This is the sexiest thing I've ever seen on you," he whispered as he met her eye. "Seeing it today, seeing you today, doing your thing, saving my brother. Baby, you're fucking magnificent. And you choose to be fucking mine. I am the luckiest son of a bitch."

She swore she saw his eyes welling up with tears, which made the backs of her own eyes burn, threatening to shed tears. Blinking, she tried to will them away. "Dash—"

He placed a finger on her lips. "Daniel," he said before sliding his finger away and kissing her softly with a gentle emotion she felt in every fiber of her being. "Only for you. Call me Daniel. My brothers call me Dash, but you, my woman, mine, call me Daniel."

That did it. She couldn't swallow them down. She couldn't blink them away. They fell. One from each eye. "Daniel."

He smiled and stroked her hair. "I have something for you," he said before kissing her forehead and leaning back.

Swiping the tears away, she watched him go to the closet. Nothing in her romantic history prepared her for meeting Daniel. He challenged her and defied everything she thought she knew. He kept her off balance but never allowed her to fall, so she felt safe around him despite being a dangerous man in a dangerous world.

"In the biker world," he said with his back to her. "When a guy finds a woman, his woman, a woman that he doesn't want to share, that he commits to, he declares her his Ol' Lady. The club considers her his property."

Her fingers trailed along the silver ring around her neck. "Sounds familiar."

A short chuckle came from him. "It's a big fucking deal to be an Ol' Lady," he said before turning and showing her a small vest, a woman's vest, with patches sewed on it. The top arched patch read, "Property of" and the bottom one read, "Dash."

She peered up at him.

Then he turned it and she saw the lapel had a rectangular patch sewn onto it. It read, "Gingersnap."

She gasped and covered her mouth while new tears streamed down her face.

"I only get one Ol' Lady," he said as he closed the distance between them. "And you're mine. Your collar declares you're mine in the BDSM community. This property vest will tell everyone else you're mine."

There weren't any words. He once again overwhelmed her in his very Dash way.

He returned to his knees before her. "Take off your shirt and bra."

Without a moment's hesitation, she peeled her shirt over her head. She tossed it to a corner somewhere. Reaching behind her, she unhooked her bra, tugged it down her arms, and that too was cast aside. She was just as eager as he was to have the leather against her skin.

The second he slid it on, she shuddered. Her nipples stiffened into pebbled peaks and her body heated. It was a new vest—stiff and cool against her body. She ran her fingers along the bottom before she met his eyes. "I love it."

He grinned before nestling back before her. "You look perfect."

Digging his fingers into her ass, he lifted her before tossing her onto the bed. He reached for the button of her jeans and undid her fly. Since he forgot about shoes, she kicked them off. He tugged down her jeans and growled, seeing her panties.

"Didn't we discuss this?" he asked.

A flush heated her body, more than it already had been. "Yes," she murmured, trying to squeeze her thighs together.

His hand cracked against her thigh and the sting shot through her core like a bolt of lightning to her sex. She cried out as he yanked her panties down. With one hand he massaged her sex, the other he worked at his own jeans.

"As punishment, I'm going to have to forgo my plan and rush to the good part."

She smiled as he climbed over her. The weight of his body on her caused her to shudder. There wasn't a feeling in the world better than being under a powerful, dominant man. He pushed her vest open, exposing her breasts.

She gasped when the wet heat covered her nipple. She hissed her inhale and arched her body. Everything he did had her squirming and wanting more of him. The fire of need burned deep within her and he fanned the flames as he teased her breast with licks and bites.

"Please," she begged.

Her eyes widened as her breath left her lungs. The feel of his cock pressing against her pussy, filling her with every inch of his thickness, drew all of her attention. He took it slowly, making sure they both savored every moment.

With his arms on either side of her head, he met her gaze. His cock fully seated in her sex, she tried to grind against him. "Mine," he growled before he leaned down to take her bottom lip between his teeth. She whimpered, needing him to move more.

Dash bucked his hips as the nip to her lip turned into a desperate, needy kiss. Slowly, he dragged his cock back before pushing it deep inside her again. Squirming beneath him, she reveled in the feel of his body weight over her—not enough to crush her, but just enough pressure to remind her to stay where he wanted her.

He overwhelmed every one of her senses with his. He surrounded her—he tasted her—he was all she could feel and could focus on. This was what it meant to be possessed. This was what she'd been looking for. She finally found it in Dash, and Liz would do everything she could to keep this feeling.

Soft and sweet. He took his time. She'd always laughed at the idea of calling sex 'making love,' but that night, she finally understood what that meant. She'd been falling in love with him since their first scene. This night, with their bodies joined in the tender way they made love, she couldn't stop the words from spilling past her lips.

"I love you," she whispered before she fell over the cliff of an orgasm after he'd driven himself deep into her.

"I love you," he repeated, making her heart swell that much more.

EPILOGUE

Dash

The cards dealt. The river turned. Drinks poured. Women in laps. Seriously, this was the dream. When he'd pictured what his life would be like once he'd joined and got settled, this was it. Lifting the corner of his cards seeing the king and two, he snorted and shook his head. Okay, in his dream scenario he had a better hand. He threw his cards away.

Then again, he grinned as his other hand ran up and down Liz's thigh, he did have something better than a winning poker hand.

Looking over her shoulder, she smiled. Leaning back, she offered him a sweet kiss before she turned back to the table of his brothers.

Tomorrow Romeo and Sparrow would go home. They'd go back to the mother chapter without him. They'd leave Whiskey behind, the only blight on this perfect send off – their brother recuperating. If he could curb stomp Tut and Jackal just to see their jaws rip from their heads and hear their pain, he'd be a happy man. He hated the idea of his brother, a good man, suffering because of them. They wouldn't know loyalty if it were crammed down their fucking throats.

"Okay, I have a question." Liz's statement tore him from his murderous thoughts and drew his focus. Her gaze drifted from one of his brothers to another. "What's with the nicknames?"

"Road names, Cher." Cajun corrected as he pointed his cards at her then tossed them away indicating he folded.

"There's a difference?" Dash's woman asked.

The men around the card table chuckled. A round of checks and calls went around the table.

Sparrow rolled her eyes. "No," she offered. "They're the same thing. They just get their panties in a bunch about it."

Dash lifted his shoulder. "It's a biker thing." He wasn't about to get into road name versus nickname. As far as he was concerned they were essentially semantics at her level.

Liz nodded. "Okay." She again looked around. "So, how do you get them?"

"Your sponsor gives it to you," Romeo answered as he handed out cards to the remaining players.

As Dash absentmindedly ran his fingers along the back of Liz's neck, she tilted her head giving him more access. "Do they mean anything?"

"Sometimes," he said. "Other times they're just funny." He paid particular attention to the bold, shiny, steel ring she wore – the collar he'd given her.

"What about yours?" she asked.

Sparrow burst out laughing. "I still don't know how he got his." She thumbed toward Romeo. "And quite frankly, I'm not sure I want to. I mean, Romeo." She rolled her eyes in exaggeration. "I can only imagine."

Dash quirked a brow and cocked his head to the side.

"You never told her?" He was surprised the young biker hadn't shared that tidbit with his woman.

When the dark haired man gave a nonchalant shrug in response, Dash shook his head and tsk'ed.

"I'll tell you since I'm his sponsor and all." He dropped his hand so that he could wrap both around his own woman. He felt an urge to hold her tighter. "He had it bad for you. And it reminded me of that Shakespeare play, Romeo and Juliet. You know with the whole two different clubs and star crossed lovers pining for each other bullshit. Yeah, he got that name cause of you, Lollipop Girl." Dash winked. "You're his Juliet and he's Romeo."

"Oh my God," the women said in unison. "That's so sweet."

"You think you could get your pussy off the table so we can play cards, Cher?" Cajun asked.

"You're not even in the hand," Sparrow snapped before she snuggled against Romeo.

Dash chortled. Liz shifted in his lap to face him. He could see the question in her eyes before she asked it. "Is yours as romantic?"

Pulling one of his hands back, he stroked his beard. "Nah," he admitted. "Tex isn't as sentimental as I am. Or, not in the same way I guess."

She furrowed her brow in confusion.

"Tex, my dad, was his sponsor," Romeo offered in between Sparrow kisses.

Liz nodded in understanding.

"I'm an army vet," Dash said.

"I knew that." His woman puffed out her chest in pride.

He grinned. "When I prospected with Odin's Fury, I made it a point to learn all by-laws and protocols and everything. I wanted to make sure I didn't fuck up. You know how important rules are to me." He lifted his brows.

Her smile took on a mischievous undertone.

"In the army, technical manuals, which are the closest thing to a user or an owner's manual in the civilian world, are called dash tens. When Tex saw how well I knew the club by-laws, he started calling me Dash Ten. Eventually, he just shortened it to Dash."

She frowned.

"What?"

"It's not as cute."

He laughed and wrapped her in a hug. "Maybe not to you."

"Mais la! Fuck and get it over with," Cajun sighed. "I just want to play cards or see something worth watching."

NOTE FROM AUTHOR

Thank you for enjoying this journey with me and my characters. Authors love reviews. If you enjoyed this book, please consider leaving a review on Goodreads or your website of choice. If you would like to be the first to hear about my latest news, please click here to sign up to my author newsletter or go here: https://www.authorvictoria jayne.com/newsletter-signup. I send them out periodically for updates on my new releases, book recommendations, special offers, and/or exclusive content.

Newsletter Sign Up

ALSO BY VICTORIA JAYNE

Follow me on Amazon:

https://www.amazon.com/stores/Victoria-Jayne/author/
B07KXJH13F

The Prophecy Trilogy:

The Witch of the Prophecy

The Wolf of the Prophecy

The Vampire of the Prophecy

Odin's Fury Motorcycle Club Series:

Jacob

Sparrow

Dash

Gingersnap

Mooky

Blue

Romeo – FREE Bonus Chapter

Elemental Dragon Series:

Giving the Dragon Fire

Giving the Dragon an Invitation - FREE Bonus Chapter

Giving the Dragon Ice

Giving the Dragon Water

Giving the Dragon Freedom

Dixie Mafia Series:

Fling of Hearts (Novella in Charity Anthology)

Queen of Blades

Standalone:

Hot Mess Honey

ABOUT THE AUTHOR

Victoria Jayne is a Jersey Girl through and through. She doesn't pump gas, she eats pork roll, and grew up on the shore. She lives with her journalist husband and her two darling daughters.

When not writing, Victoria enjoys baking with her daughters, rooting for the New Jersey Devils, thinking of home improvement projects for her husband, daydreaming/planning vacations she'll never take, and staying up far too late chatting on Discord.

The worlds of Suzanne Wright, JD Tyler, Dianne Duvall, Elisabeth Naughton, Madeline Sheehan, Tillie Cole, Kim Jones, JL Drake, and Joanne Wylde inspired Victoria. After binge reading them, she committed to writing and publishing her own books. She loves discovering new authors and the characters they create just as much as her own.